Published in 2010 by Prion
An imprint of the Carlton Publishing Group
20 Mortimer Street
London W1T 3JW

Copyright © 2010 Carlton Books Limited

All rights reserved. This book is sold subject to the condition that it may not be reproduced, stored in a retrieval system or transmitted in any form or by any means, electronic, mechanical, photocopying, recording or otherwise without the publisher's prior consent.

A CIP catalogue record for this book is available from the British Library.

ISBN 978 1 85375 797 6

Printed in the UK by CPI Mackays, Chatham, ME5 8TD

10 9 8 7 6 5 4 3 2 1

# YOU DON'T KNOW... JACK SCHITT

## THE PRIVATE EYE WHO DOESN'T TAKE ANY CRAP

### NIKO BESLEY

PRION

## Chapter 1: The Postman Always Rings Twice

```
The broad had fallen gracefully. Sprawled
on the kitchen floor, she could have been
advertizing the latest in parquet flooring - if
it wasn't for the gaping one-inch hole in her
alabaster forehead. My eyes skimmed the joint.
Not a thing out of place except the glass of
wine she'd been holding (an afternoon drinker,
I noted) smashed on the floor beside her. The
Scene of Crime Investigator tenderly knelt by
her, and then looked up.
```

"A single shot from a .38, I'm guessing a TC Encore, detective. Can't give you much more than that at the moment."

She was a good-time girl, who seemed to have a few admirers on simmer without wanting to bring any of them to the boil. Could be any one of those schmucks. The execs wouldn't stand a few minutes rock'n'roll, but that nightclub owner looked like he could handle himself.

The phone rang. Damn. This was one of the few *Houston: Forensic Unit* episodes I hadn't seen. It was probably Mr Ballowski wanting to know if I'd check again on whether Marilyn Monroe was his biological mother, or maybe my own Ma checking if I'd eaten my pastrami on rye yet. I looked at the call ident. Number

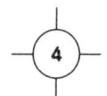

Withheld. I let it ring. The answerphone summoned the energy to click and whirr.

"Jack Schitt, Private Investigator – If you've got something to say, say it and hang up."

I waited for whatever flotsam was about to float my way. I'd seen pretty much all the low life, trailer trash and god-fearing citizens that Mazomanie, Wisconsin could muster in the way of investigation – missing dogs, employment histories, hookey insurance claims, messy divorces – but I couldn't afford to turn it down. The Mid-West had been getting along pretty fine for too long without a private dick with a nose for the truth.

"Er... Jack... It's..." Then gone. I stared at the phone trying to place that voice. It was calm, assured, not like the hysterical calls I get screaming for justice, revenge and a ten per cent discount as mentioned in the ad in the *Mazomanie Trumpet*. But this reticent punter knew my name. I began to run through the mug shots in the "customer" file of my mind.

After 20 long years of tailing, sniffing around and writing reports, I'd seen them all come and go, the pimps, junkies, Johns, loons, hustlers and players, wise guys and smart girls. Unfortunately I'd have to walk on by them to the realty agents, insurance salesman, bank tellers and dowdy homemakers whose turgid cases paid just enough to get me a two-roomed apartment, a limited supply of corn juice and a General Tso's chicken from Singapore Sam's on a Friday night.

Yep. I sure wasn't living the dream. Just what did Phillip Marlowe, Sam Spade or Mike Hammer have that I was missing? Pound for pound, I could duke it out with any of those guys. I talked the talk, walked the walk and, if it hadn't been for the

## Chapter 1

unfortunate incident at the target practice, I'd be packing my own piece now. Maybe it was time to take up smoking again. I reached for the pack that still sat on the desk. It had been crying for attention like a six year old in a divorce court. Just one for now, I promised myself. Before I could light it, the phone sang again.

And the voice came back: "Mike Snarling. You might remember me, Jack; we had some dealings a few years back. Give me a call – room 1178, Bellevue Hotel, Hollywood."

My office is what you'd call compact. You might also call it the living room. Stretching back on the chair I could reach the grey metal filing cabinet that contained my life's work. Filing wasn't my strong point and the dozy intern I'd been sent from the local librarian college had neatly rearranged my mess of papers into a Dewey decimal system. I tried 550 Earth Sciences, 640 Home Economics and Family Living and 240 Christian Moral & Devotional Theology where I was briefly distracted by a case involving a vicar, a stable boy and 200lbs of thoroughbred filly.

Detectives are no different to the rest of the slobbering ranks of massed humanity, so I did what any fourth-grader stuck on their homework would do. I Googled my caller. In 0.06 seconds came an answer – Jesus H, no wonder no one needs a private dick any more, it takes me three times as long as that to do up my zipper. From three million results, I picked a familiar site: "Born November 1960, Mike Snarling is a music executive, TV producer and right smart ass. Famous for lighting his own farts, managing fatuous boy bands without a single brain cell and shoving rotting vegetables up his own crack, his smug, smarmy face is due a pummelling for daring to besmirch this otherwise beautiful planet."

Aaah Wikipedia! The truly democratic way of bringing someone down a peg or two. It was probably as near to the truth as the other more polite biogs that spoke of this humble record executive whose TV pop talent shows had brought him management deals, overnight sensation bands who he'd manage to a hit single before dumping them and breakfast cereal endorsements – all amounting to enough dollars to wallpaper the White House.

But what would Mr Billionaire TV man want with a hick dick with all the schtick like me? I clicked through more sites: "Snarling launches inner-city drugs rehabilitation centre", "Snarling joins Prince William on yacht", "Snarling divorces after ten years of 'great times'". Then a name caught my eye – Lucy Snarling. Mark's now ex had reverted to her maiden name, Spight. The Spights were an old-time Mazomanie family. I delved through my whisky-soaked sponge that passes for a brain. As a young Turk up for anything, I'd done old man Spight's debt-claiming. I'd also taken roll after roll of Miriam Spight making out in the back of a Chevvy with a married tree stump remover... suddenly it came to me: Jimmy the Fence!

Little Lucy Spight had grown up and settled for a DJ on the local airwaves – I was always a late-night jazz man myself. Five people all playing a different tune and making a darned awful racket, ain't that a little like life? Incoherent nonsense but it seemed the kind of thing a hard-boiled detective should like and it usually sent me to sleep eventually. But her guy, Mark, was Drive Time: traffic, light news, sport and bubble gum pop – I never listened to him, at least not until he paid me 500 green

## Chapter 1

ones to sort out a little problem he was having.

I don't go looking for trouble, and the truth is I rarely find it. Most folk take a polite request, a stern look or a letter from the legals and the whole deal's as easy as duck soup. But when it's time to make some chin music, I can hit on all eight. Jimmy the Fence was a case in point. He was off the track and when it came to put the screws on, I showed the dube who was chef and who was eggplant-chopping.

So Lucy and her guy, Mark, got their rhino and I earned myself a reputation as bonafide shamus – all be it one with a broken schnozzle. But while I gumshoed my way around Assholeville for years, Mr Mark seemed to have trotted up that yellow brick road to La La Land. I hadn't even noticed he was gone and now here he was some Hollywood big shot. Some guys, some luck, eh?

It wouldn't do to call the Jasper straight back. I looked at the pack of charch and felt my insides churn like a teenager on the waltzer. "Later," I hissed at them and took myself off – O'Mallogans, Mazomanie's finest hooch house, had been open for five minutes and it didn't seem right to leave it waiting.

## Chapter 2: Career in C Minor

```
My eyelids felt like hundred-pound weights as I
dead-lifted them open to squint at the clock.
It was six in the morning, but the guys with
the jackhammers inside my head still hadn't
knocked off. A cup of Joe hid the taste of
stale liquor but a left foot up the guava from
the Mazomanie Mohawks place-kicker would barely
get me moving.
```

Drink – it was an occupational hazard. I hated the stuff, but a teetotal private eye? Like a straight air steward – you'd get no trust. This is the oil that lubricates our business – that and the rough stuff. At least this way I only end up with a hangover. So I cleaned up, scraped away a couple of day's stubble, poured a bucketful of morning mud down me and crawled back to my desk.

The answerphone was still winking at me. Mark Spight, or whatever his name was, had called back. I bashed out the number on the hotel website and got transferred to his room.

"Snarling."
"Schitt."
"Wrong number?"
"No, Schitt."
"No shit?"

## Chapter 2

"No. Jack Schitt."

"Ahh Jack – I've been waiting for you to call." Quite obviously, I thought.

"Remember me, Jack? You used to do my burgers real crispy."

"I quit BonzoBurger in 1975."

"Good burgers though. You really don't remember me?"

"Nope." These famous dudes really think they've always walked around with a halo. "I recall Jimmy the Fence though," I added.

"Hmm. Nasty business that. How is the nose?"

"I can whistle through it on a good day."

"I want to make it up to you, Jack. You took a big one for me that day. You busy?"

"There's always some schmuck wants someone followed."

"Get yourself out here, Jack. There's a ticket waiting for you down at C-Way."

I'm never inclined to give in to a client too easily – even when there's a one-wayer down to the Sunshine state. But LA – where all the gumshoes go to die – was difficult to turn down.

"I've a few decks to deal," I answered. "I'll see what I can do."

"You know the song, Jack, 'Go West – Life is peaceful there...'" And he hung up.

LAX – not so much an airport as a statement. It shouts welcome to the peak of the great American dream; the sum of all the futile plans, crazy ambitions and impossible aspirations of every punk on the continent. It's LA, Uncle Sam's paradise garden of glamour, bright lights, beautiful bodies and seven-day-a-week sunshine.

It was raining. And I thanked the Lord it was an airport as well as a statement as I was dying for the John by the time my flight landed. I'd found the driver in the arrivals lounge trying to avoid revealing his A4 piece of paper with the word "Shit" written on it. To the soundtrack of some awful mariachi band from deepest LA Central, my cab took off.

"Friend of Mr Snarling?" he asked, as I took off my hat and settled in for the ride. I didn't reply.

"He said to look after you real well, sir," he added.

Then it hit me like a really difficult equation to a shit-hot math professor – no one knows me here. Just like those bottle blondes, glistening-faced boys and the movie writers who put an "i" on the end of their names to sound more Italian, I can be whoever I want. And I was going to be a private dick so hardboiled that it'd take a sledgehammer to bust my shell and even then it would be pretty tough to separate the yolk from the white.

"Jack Schitt's nobody's possum, uncle. I've got one mom, she's back in Wisconsin running a Unity Church coffee morning and until someone tells me she's gone to see the chuck she does the gratis work for, I'm not advertising for another."

"Yessir," replied straight-outta-Juarez, looking a little puzzled. "Mr Snarling has booked you in to the Palace Hotel in Beverley Hills. He said he'll see you in his office at 3.00."

"Take me downtown."

"Sir? The Palace Hotel is the best in the city; six stars and you've got the penthouse – Michael Jackson, Prince Charles, Beyoncé, Stephen Hawking, they all stay there.

For a moment, I was wrong-footed. Clean sheets, mini bar, cable TV and those little chocolates they put on your pillow. Club

## Chapter 2

sandwiches on room service and a free dressing gown and slippers. Sure beats the three-month old sheets and mouldy leftovers in the fridge that I was used to. But I'd come here to work.

"You know a motel downtown, a sleaze joint where even the roaches have checked out?"

"Sounds like my cousin's place, sir. But I don't think Mr Snarling would..."

"And, I don't think Mr Snarling would want you to upset me."

Ramirez was a good guy, just doing the best he could. His cousin Benny wasn't so friendly for a businessman who looked pretty desperate for a customer who would book a room by the week rather than by the hour. He flashed an insincere toothless grin, took my money and flung a rusty old key at me. The key ring bore the legend "Arcadia Motel – enjoy your stay in the City of Angels" – on the reverse it read "Sponsored by Hi-Jean Syringe Bank – clean needles save lives".

Room 43 was no penthouse suite. The door hardly needed a lock; I could have blown it open, if I had enough breath left after the eight flights of stairs. The light from a tiny prison cell window struggled to fill the room, but I could still see the washed-out blood stains on the carpet. One single bed, a wardrobe only kept vertical by a pile of Gideon bibles and a sink with a cracked mirror. I took a deep breath and took in the fetid aroma of grime, body odour and 99 cent air freshener. It felt like home.

The face of the grunt in the mirror didn't look out of place here. It had an equally badly lived-in look. But beneath the greying at the sides, the tired eyes, the emerging nasal hair, the uneven stubble, the crooked snoot and the square jaw, there was a street-brawler, a man whose only ambition was to get to the truth – although, come to think of it, he wouldn't mind getting laid soon as well. And a few greenbacks could come in handy.

"Thank You for Not Smoking" said the sticker above the ashtray, still full of butts from the last 17 punters. I took a stick from the pack and hung it from the corner of my lips. I looked back in the mirror: "Put the metal down brother – it's not polite to point it." I practised: "If those pants get any tighter they'd be on the inside, baby doll"... I spun round to the half-opened door. There stood Benny, ill-advisedly leaning on the frame, shaking his head, his grin breaking into a full-on cackle.

I splashed some water, grabbed my hat and made for the hills. The Hollywood hills. I waited outside Benny's for a hack for the best part of an hour before joining the gumstretchers and gagas on the bus. Half an hour pulling elbows out of my ribs, avoiding the stares of the homeboys and wondering what the wet patch I'd sat on was. But, at last I was working the big one – LA. I pulled my collar up and put the hat on – people needed to know there was a new sheriff in town. The woman sitting next to me edged further along the seat. Either she'd noticed the aura or that wet patch was what I thought it was.

It was a tough calling being a gumshoe, an op, a private dick, a ticket carrier. We're not like ordinary Joes – We sit outside of society, find it hard to form relationships with either sex and are looked on with suspicion – a bit like PE teachers. But where you rarely meet a sharp-tongued PE teacher, your PI needs to have a quick answer at the ready. It's no good ringing the hustler two hours later with a killer line you've thought of on the train on the way home. Then there's the lingo – everyone thinks they know it

## Chapter 2

from the film patter: dames, broads, who's putting the screws on and who's been pooped – but there's books full of the stuff, it's tougher than French.

Mark had an office at TBA Television Studios. It was an old movie lot first put up in the days when Chaplin, Keaton and that other guy with a moustache would take over a barn and churn out three movies a week to be lapped up by noddies around the world. Now it was a glass and metal hamster wheel for tight skirts and designer suits.

The uniform at the gate didn't like the look of me. I couldn't blame him. A crumpled raincoat and three days of stubble didn't serve as an ID card in many places now. But Snarling's name was big berries in this business and he couldn't afford to cut too much beef on me. A mumble or two into his walkie-talkie and he sent me walking to the lobby.

I got swallowed by the big red sofa and took in the gleaming teeth of TBA's big stars. They were giant posters, but none of these chippies and gunsels were worth the shoe leather of a Jimmy Cagney, John Wayne or Phil Silvers. Still Brad whoever and Tiffany whateverhername looked down on me like Zeus and his chick from Mount Olympus. I caught the broad behind the desk cast a stare down her nose like a bowling ball. Yes, I wanted to tell her, they're called shoes, not everyone has to dress like they've come straight from school sports day.

I was over an hour late but Snarling was in no evident rush to see me. I took out my burns and shook them. They were still packed in as tight as ten little Indian boys – except there were twenty.

"Mr err?" the bowling alley queen looked down at my name on her list and thought better of it. "No smoking please sir."

I could wait. Behind her, a figure emerged from the elevator. Tall, slender build with a French crop. A few years in this business and you soon develop a knack of instantly knowing who are the puppets and just who are pulling the strings.

"Snarling?" I growled.

"Not me I'm afraid," a fey voice shot back. "He's just coming though." And he sashayed his way out the building.

"Jack!" The boom of authority shook the room. And he came striding towards me hand outstretched. Tall, medium build, perma-tanned and a French crop, Snarling had a white tee under his green Fioravanti suit, his trousers strangely hitched up almost as far as his armpits. He smiled sanctimoniously It was a look that instantly said I can buy you and all the little ants on your mound with my spare change. Right away I didn't take to the man but if I ditched every chit on account of the smell, I'd play a lot more chess.

His office was white. Whiter than white. I mentally tossed up whether to let him know that Martha Stewart had told us it was time to move on to some primary colours, but somehow felt our relationship needed to develop first. Snarling was all pleasantries, coffee and old times.

"After Jimmy the Fence, I thought things had looked up for you, Jack? Apart from the nose business, of course. But I guess it didn't work out."

"I'm working."

"Fifty dollar jobs some hoodlum kid with his ass hanging out his trousers could manage. You're better that that Jack. Did they straighten it at hospital or did you do it yourself."

"Drop the schnozzle rap, Snarling," I snapped. "I'm a Jake – I

## Chapter 2

stroll for the Hamiltons, just give me the ticket or I breeze."

"Are you for real?" the cat laughed. "Listen Jack, it's cool. Have a drink, relax and try to speak 21st century, can't you. No one gets that Bogart stuff anymore."

Smiling, he handed me a large Jack Daniels. "You want it straight like Hammer or on the rocks like Spade?"

"Do you have any Canadian Club?" And he thought he had me figured!

"Twelve years ago I left that bunghole you call home. You know getting out of Mazomanie was the best thing I ever did, Jack." Mark leaned back in his easy chair. What was it about every client that made them think you wanted their life story? I thought to myself. I'm a private dick who wants facts and numbers not some budget-rate shrink who needs to know what your teddy was called or that you still wet the bed when the Dodgers lose.

"I managed a band, learned to handle a production desk, got myself an office in the record company and poked my nose in a few places it didn't belong. I saw where the real bucks were being made and elbowed my way in. There are some scary faces in this town but they all carry a change of underwear – if you get my drift."

"Good line," I thought. "I'll write that down when I get back to El Cucaracha."

"And I remembered those old Seventies talent shows like *Reach for the Stars* and *New Faces* and thought just maybe it's time to bring them up to date. I added a little sex, a little bump and grind, some r'n'b and watched what happened? Kazam! *You Got What It Takes?*" America's most popular light entertainment programme, the show that brought you Little Marlon, LaQuinta and XTINCT Featuring Stinkee-D.

"Never heard of any of them." Frank, Dean, Ella and Billie, I thought. Who needed anything else?

"It was a good recipe, Snarling. Made you a stack of dough."

"You could say that, Jack. I've a mansion in Beverley Hills that used to belong to Rock Hudson, a cabin in Aspen and a few bolt holes in Europe. I could walk away from it all today and never have to lift a finger again. But you know why I don't?"

I shrugged.

"Because I can't. It's an addiction. Sure I love the money, the attention, the fame – but, I'll be honest with you Jack and it doesn't sound good. What I couldn't live without is the electricity of what I do. I make these kids dreams come true – to them I'm Jesus, Willy Wonka and the genie of the lamp all stuffed into a pair of Armani leather trousers."

Snarling finished his spiel and gave me a half smile and a hard stare. I wanted to puke. When I'd looked up Mr Bigstuff on the worldwide, half the people wanted to punch him in the face, half just wanted to tell him to wear lower-waisted pants but all admired his blarney. I felt like he just spread his oozing chutzpah over my face and I couldn't wait to wash it off.

"So what made you haul me in from Mazomonie, Candyman?" I fixed his stare with one of my own – well one I borrowed from Jimmy Stewart in *Call Northside 777*. "I'm getting on a bit for your boy bands and though I pass muster with a reasonably decent *Fly Me to the Moon* the song lacks the booty, bitches and butts for today's hit parade."

"Too right. You're certainly not here for your good looks, Schitt," he laughed. "But I need a bit of that Jack Schitt attitude plus I figured

## Chapter 2

it's someone else's turn to use that stool at the bar in O'Mallogans!"

Then he put on a serious face – like he was going to tell me my mother had died. And I still hadn't called her.

"I got a job for you, Jack. One I thought you'll be good at. Some of my kids here have been getting a little hassle. A warning here; an accidental fall there. Nothing too serious, but I like a happy camp, Jack. Someone's bringing their grubby little practices into my little Shangri-La and I don't like it."

At least my mother was OK. "Why not bring in the coffee and doughnuts?"

"Sorry? You hungry? I'll call..."

"The badges? The elbows? The size twelves?" He cocked his head in that irritating way I had watched him do on HYGWIT? on Youtube – just before he laid into someone.

"You mean the police? God no! It'll be all over the tabloids in no time. It's probably a storm in a teacup anyway. The competition gets pretty hot in that studio. Maybe it's someone's brother getting a little over protective or a misguided friend?"

"Or a mob on a gambling fix?"

"Don't go all Edward G already Jack, like I said it's not heavy."

"Why me though, Snarling? There must be a thousand rent-a-dicks in this city?"

"I owed you one, Jack. Jimmy the Fence, your hooter, you know the deal. And, like I said before, I get a kick out of making dreams come true. A detective in the big city, that's your dream, isn't it, Jack? I thought I'd get you the big break and well, like I say in the show, 'Have you got what it takes?'"

# Chapter 3: Sweet Smell of Success

---

```
The next evening I was back at the studio. I'd
made Snarling sweat for as long as I could but
when he went to his safe and started counting
piles of the Federal bank's promises, he knew
I'd take the ticket. Maybe it was a dirty job
in a dirty city but I was the man who'd been
given the pan and brush.
```

I'd come to see the show. I hadn't realized how big the thing was. It was the quarter-finals and even a couple of hours before recording there were hundreds of pre-pubes hanging around, waiting for a glimpse of their idols. Everyone was so excited; it felt like a Jehovah's Witness convention where Jesus was billed as the main speaker. And, on top of this, Snarling had reckoned on thirty million or so viewers settling down to watch the six fresh face wannabes live on TV.

    I thought I'd keep my head down, stay unnoticed and take in the scene. I stood near the back of the studio where I could get a good view of proceedings. The seats gradually filled with hordes of screaming, hysterical families from every corner of the nation, all dressed in brightly coloured T-shirts with the mug of their particular favourite splattered across the chest. In my raincoat and homburg I stood out like a virgin's Johnson in a brothel.

## Chapter 3

Snarling had got me VIP tickets. I was down the front with the families of the contestants. I squeezed into the part of my seat that wasn't occupied by the overflowing flab of the 20-plus stone woman next to me. On the other side ten members of a family were standing up and chanting in unison. Each of them was holding up a letter: I craned my neck round but could only get as far as F-E-L-L-A-T-I. I smiled at the young woman on my left and managed to catch the badge fixed to her left shoulder. On it was scribbled: "Sister of Fellatiana". Nice.

I felt myself jammed into her as Grimace turned to talk at me.

"Who you with?" she spat at me.

"I'm undecided," I told her. "A floating voter."

"Not any more," she announced as she stuck a huge badge across my chest. I peered down to discover I was now a "Friend of Jasmira".

Four hours later I was free. The singers had been OK – they had sung in duets in some kind of mock camaraderie; they'd each sung a Motown classic which had been watered down, cut short and surgically removed of any charm the original had claimed and finally they had sung their own choice of song – without fail a soppy r'n'b ballad. Then came the real torture time. A talentless bunch of has-beens, known as "the celebrity panel" assessed each of the performances. Alternately humiliating them or heralding them as the new Caruso, they gave the great American public a clue as to who they should vote for and keep in the competition.

Meanwhile, the audience were driven from extreme excitement to pant-wetting euphoria. I got up and shouted along, doing my bit for Jasmira – mainly on account of Big Mama putting my arm in a Chinese grip and fearing she might sit on me if I didn't give her baby my full support.

Special guest for the night had been Venice Budgetlodge. Venice was famously famous for being famous. Once an heiress to her daddy's economy motel empire, the old man had now written her out on account of some footage leaked onto the internet involving her, two fellas, no clothes and an excited dachshund. It had been the final straw and now he wouldn't even pay her manicure bills.

A tabloid heroine or monster, depending which day of the week it was – she had been giving the contestants lessons in "Media Awareness" and had come back to report on her charges. She also "delighted us" with a song from her new album which made you feel she was lucky daddy had bought her a recording studio and she didn't have to compete on the show herself.

I got up and stretched. My ears were ringing and my empathy gauge was in the red. It had been a real sentiment fest: a rollercoaster of manufactured anguish, elation, togetherness, rivalry, bitter criticism, boundless acclamation, triumph and, for Fellatiana and a soppy 14-year-old boy (who you suspected would now be beaten up daily by his schoolmates) a heartbreaking tragedy. Everyone was in tears. Whether it was from disappointment, ecstasy or in response to the pathetic levels to which humankind could sink it was hard to tell.

Escaping the crowds I headed for the green room as Snarling had instructed. This was me clocking in for a shift at the coal face. He'd told the kids and the others on the show that he'd brought me in for their security, that I was an experienced

## Chapter 3

detective who'd act with discretion. He told me to get to know them, have a sniff around and see if anything wasn't coming up Yves Saint Laurent.

The room was buzzing. I shouldered my way through ageing soul singers in sparkling dresses and dressed-down rock stars whose hits live on but whose names have long been forgotten, and grabbed a glass of champagne.

"Hey Jack! I see you made a friend already!" Snarling was pointing at the sticker still emblazoned across my chest. I went to pull it off.

"Don't be too hasty... maybe you'll like me after all!" a voice purred, as sweet and smooth as honey.

Jasmira towered above me. Six foot something in her heels. She flicked her long black hair and modestly tugged down her tight red and black dress to try to cover another inch of her thighs. Snarling introduced me and slid off.

"I'm so glad that's over," she said blowing an imaginary puff over my head.

"You were great," I lied. So this is what Snarling had got me in for, babysitting a bunch of kindergarten crooners.

I tried her with some small talk but she surprised me. She was funny, intelligent and was happy to take the whole thing as a game. And when I apologized for not being able to remember any of her performances that night, she said she understood and that she'd have equal trouble telling me apart from all the other detectives she'd met.

The rest of the evening spun by as I met all the remaining contenders: Stephen, a bushy-haired boy channelling the spirit of Justin Timberlake; Melrose, a beautiful God-fearing gospel singer from Tennessee; white rapper Marko, fresh out of a top drawer English public school; Dwayne T, a boy band veteran already with his own record contract; and ten-year-old protégée Roxy, accompanied by her mother but already ten times more savvy than the rest of them.

I'd done my job for the day. Worked out who's who and who wanted what. All except one. I'd noticed the motel dame flinging glances at me all night. And I didn't think she was after knowing who my tailor was. If I turned to catch her eye, she'd turn back to one of her adoring crowd. But I had a bigger hunch than Quasimodo that she'd be talking to me sooner or later.

As the party emptied I finally caught up with Snarling. "Great kids, eh?" He smarmed at me. "I wish they could all win." It was then I heard someone call my name. "Schitt!"

## Chapter 4: Leave Her to Heaven

"Schitt! Holy Shit - help!" I ran back along the corridor followed by the rest of the party stragglers. In the half-opened door to the dressing room Jasmira was screaming like a banshee on a rollercoaster. Either she'd broken a fingernail or it was time Jack Schitt earned his scraps. I eased her aside and stepped into the room. There, flung in the corner was a blue dress - with a body still in it. I tippitoed towards it.

"You OK, babe?" I whispered.

"Of course she's not OK. She's dead, Schitt! Christ!"

Twenty-five years a private dick and I'd never seen a dead body before. Dead dogs, bums sleeping in the gutters, broads passing out in the noonday, but never a real stiff. How do you know if they've really checked out? I didn't want to touch her but everyone was looking at me like I was House MD so I grabbed her wrist and felt for a pulse. Nothing. The dame had bitten the big one.

I loosened my tie, gulped for breath and tried to pull myself together. Means of death? Come on, Schitt. Clues? Marks on the body? I looked again at her face, cold and dull eyes staring into the distance. I felt distinctly woozy, like chucking out time at O'Mallogans.

Could she really be getting up and reaching up to me. But she was dead... As the room spun round, I grasped the truth too late. It was me who was going down, sinking on top of her in a slow faint.

I came to and saw Snarling's face moving in and out of focus. He was shaking me like a can of beans.

"What the hell are you doing," he hissed. "Get off her."

I mumbled "cause of death, jet lag and not had much to eat," picked up the keys, lighter, cigs and matches that had tumbled to the ground and wiped the slobber I'd left on the broad's cheek.

Now I recognized her. It was Melrose, one of the kids on the show. Even I could tell she had talent, she could've sung the yellow pages and got a standing ovation. All night the talk had been that Melrose was the natural star of the show, tipped to win the series – "the style of Beyoncé and the voice of Aretha," Venice had pronounced at the end of the night. Now she'll be looking for St Peter to put her through to the next round. Behind me the sobbing started getting hysterical.

"Get 'em all out of here," I snapped at Snarling. "And call the buttons."

"The who?"

"The cops. She's been chilled off."

I went back to the deceased. She hadn't put up much of a fight, there was barely a hair out of place and her fingernails were intact. She almost had a smile on her face. I'd dated worse looking dames and they'd still been breathing.

"What makes you think it's murder?" asked Snarling, peering over my shoulder. I gently pulled the silk scarf from her neck and revealed the bright red sores around her neck. "Someone's given her a finger necklace and got a little too tight."

Less than 24 hours in the city and I had a dead one on my

## Chapter 4

hands already. This babysitting job had just got heavy. I thought about what Snarling had said – just a hot-headed brother throwing his weight around – had he been straight up or was he playing me?

LAPD's finest burst through the door like it was Donny Donut's on a Monday promotion.

"Hey Columbo! Get away from the body." A red-faced round detective with his shirt tails dancing behind him, flashed what looked like his bus pass at me and busied his uniforms around the place.

"You a doctor?"

"Schitt. Detective," I answered.

"This is a crime scene. Even if you're a shit-hot detective, I want you and Captain Rugrat to get the hell out of here. But don't go so far that I can't hear you fart. Now where are CSI and their test tubes?"

I woke up to the sound of a thousand Mexicans partying like it was 1810 – in my head. We'd gone back to Snarling's office to wait for the law to finish up and he'd broken out the tequila. By the time Lieutenant Somethingski got to me, I was smoked, as lit as the Vegas drag. He sent me back to Benny's in a squad car, told me to sleep it off and that he'd see me in the morning.

It was 12.30 by time I got to the central police station. Snarling was already there. He didn't look as if he'd spent the morning reliving the canapés from last night's party. A different suit, still with the trousers hoist to kingdom come, but as bushy tailed as I'd seen him.

"Shit, Schitt, you look like shit," he said. "Sorry man, I didn't realize you couldn't take your liquor – two cokes with a splash of tequila and you're falling over."

I blamed it on a dodgy filo prawn and got on with my statement. Lieutenant Chzopski wanted to know what Snarling was doing hiring a detective. I told him we used to drink out of the same bottle back in Mazomanie and he'd invited me out to see the show. I figured Snarling wouldn't want the whole intimidation thing blown wide open.

"Have you crabbed who dropped the dame yet, lieutenant?" I asked.

"Keep talking, Schitt."

"Anyone drop a dime on the killer? A sneak given you the lay?

"This is LAPD, Schitt. We talk the goddam queen's English. We don't 'crab', 'drop dimes' or 'get the lay' — whatever the bull that is. We use wires, forensics and when the CIA look the other way, some more dubious techniques — and to answer what I think is your question, yes we have a suspect."

After putting me to bed, Chzopski and his boys had worked through the night to do the same to the case. They'd lifted the boyfriend. Standard procedure with young women totings. Usually the buck ain't bad, but usually he did it — jealousy, frustration, lack of career support, whatever, it's just got too much and wham!

The CSI team had found a trace of male saliva on her cheek — unidentifiable, but enough for them to put two and two together. The bright lights had gone to the broad's head — she'd found a tastier lollipop and the boy had caught them singing from the same songbook in the dressing room. Romeo scat pronto leaving her in the hands of a kid in a red mist — or rather her neck in his hands.

The kid Chzopski had in the slammer was no hardcase. He'd been crying for his ma all night (that reminded me, I must ring mine soon, she'd be worried sick), but still hadn't fessed up. I asked Chzopski if I could have a quick word.

"Go right ahead," he smiled. "Let's see how they do it in the

## Chapter 4

mid-West, Mr Gumshoe."

The boy was cut up rough. He was no hoodlum and it seemed like he was really dizzy over the girl. So I put him on the grill and turned the heat up a little. If not him, who? He came up with deuces. Melrose had no enemies, no drug habits and, he swore, no other boyfriends – she loved God and him, in that order.

I pushed a little further – I'd heard things were getting hot in the competition; people were getting leaned on to make mistakes, hit a bum note or two. It was news to him. Melrose had told him how they'd all bonded and looked after each other. She'd been down when Venice had torn a strip off, she'd wanted to leave the show but they'd all geed her up and helped her do a great "Every Breath You Take."

He swore his innocence, saying he'd left Mel in the dressing room and just gone out to say goodbye to his folks who'd come up for the show. By the time he got back, the crowd had gathered around the doorway – he managed to squeeze in and see her lifeless body. He'd panicked, run away, trudged the streets until it was early enough to wake Father Shaunessy, who told him to give himself up and went back to bed.

I felt for the kid. I'm not saying he didn't do it, just *if* he did, he wasn't about to make a career of it. Chzopski looked smug, it was a good night's work for him and he was sure the kid would sing after a few hours of the department's TLC. I assured Chzopski that if I stumbled across anything, he'd be the first to know. He looked doubtful. He knew as well as me that Bulls and Dicks worked together about as well as Obama and the Klan.

"So long, lieutenant," I saluted as I left the station.

"Stay on the square, Peeper-Jack," he replied. And I heard the unmistakable sound of police cackle.

## Chapter 5: LA Confidential

```
I was going to have to get wise pretty quick.
Here I was in a city I felt I'd always known
every inch of - South Central, Silverlake,
Watts and the Westside out to Santa Monica,
Pacific Palisades and the canyons - yet I still
felt like a stranger in town. How did these
punks and posers live their lives?
```

I'd picked up a leaflet at Benny's. "Bugsy's LA Confidential Tours" ran a guided coach tour around the underbelly of the city. I joined it at the Staples Centre, dropping the driver ten bucks.

"Great outfit," he said. "We love it when the punters get into the spirit." I pulled my hat down and took a seat. As we set off, every turn brought new stories of murder, extortion, rackets, assassinations and bent cops. This was the city of Bugsy Siegal's protégée and successor, Mickey Cohen; of James "Two Gun" Davis; of LA godfather, Jack Dragna and of Jimmy "the Weasel" Fratianno who would eventually rat on the family.

The tourists lapped it up. Cameras clicked as we drove past the haunts of the Black Dahlia, mock executions were performed at the gutter where "The Combination" disposed of the garroted bodies of those who dared to cross it and a couple paid homage to Biggie Smalls, at the site of the rapper's execution.

## Chapter 5

"Pretty amazing eh?" said an English accent from some schmuck sitting next to me.

"Not when it's your living, brother," I replied as world weary as I could manage.

"Wow, you're a guide on one of these tours as well?"

"You could say that."

That was my cue to get off. I'd got the picture. The grime in this city wasn't going to be washed away by some glo-vest with a jet spray, it went all the way down to the sewers. And here I was in the middle of it, already with a murder to deal with. I was going to have to get my hands dirty...

I stopped at a coffee shop on Wilshire and ordered myself a double expresso. I needed to be alert. I sat outside in the sun and watched Mr and Mrs America going about their business. I took a sip of the coffee. It ran around my head, waking up every neuron that had fancied a quick sit down and 40 winks. The jolt ran down through my shoulders and flicked the switch that got my whole body buzzing. I went back to the bar.

"Do you think could you put a little hot milk in there, please."

I thought about what I had in front of me. A dead girl. A boyfriend in the tank, who didn't seem capable of getting the lid off a pickle jar, let alone strangling a healthy broad. A group of kids on the very edge of the big time. And someone making waves, though no one seemed ready to squeal yet. "You're a dick, Schitt," I told myself. "This stuff should make some sense to someone who can't open a fridge without the light coming on. I needed some inspiration. I needed to become that Schitt, I'd promised myself.

It's a truth pretty damn universally acknowledged that no self-respecting detective worth his salt is seen without a butt in his kisser. I'd tried everything – low tar, unfiltered, menthol, god-awful French ones and Moroccan sticks with a hash perfume – but they'd all leave me coughing, spluttering and puking my way along the sidewalk. But this time, I vowed, it was going to be different. I was going to make it in this town and if that meant living with a sore throat, bad breath, major organ failure and a low sperm count, so be it. I took out my pack of dugans and the book of matches and went to light up. Book? I always used a lighter, where'd the book come from? Through a foggy memory it slowly came. I'd picked it up along with the stuff that had fallen out of my pocket when I tumbled on the stiff. The book of matches must have been lying right beside her.

I rolled the book around my fingers. "The Slam Bar – The Ultimate Ultra Club, VIP luxury guaranteed". The address was in North Orange Drive in Hollywood. The matches could have been anyone's – Melrose didn't look the smoking kind, so they could have been lying on the floor where she fell or maybe they belonged to the boy in the pen. I toyed with the idea of calling Chzopski, and then thought better of it. I'd never see them again.

"When the going gets tough," I smiled to myself, "the tough go shopping." If I was to mix it with the VIP set, I was going to need some threads. I'd asked the cab driver where a man might be kitted out in style in this town. I still had some clearance on my plastic and figured Snarling would be good for some expenses. He laughed and suggested a high-class joint called Bejam out in Rodeo Drive, shopping mall of the stars. Sounded good to me.

## Chapter 5

A man used to picking his rags from thrift stores and Woolworths, I'd never seen a shop with a dummy on the door before. I had to check in as if I was being admitted to the big house. I gave him one of the 100 cards I'd had made up for five dollars at the bus station.

The number looked at the card and then back at me. "Jock Schatt – privates detective?"

OK. I'd made a couple of typos – but it got the general message over. I shrugged my shoulders.

"She's up on the fifth floor – get her out of here fast, detective – no fuss, right?"

"Jakealoo!" I nodded, heading for the lift a little confused.

What looked like a 13-year-old in an expensive suit was waiting for me on the fifth floor.

"You the detective, Schatt?" I nodded, it seemed easier. "Miss Traveller will be out in a minute. She's just running through some details with our security."

I stood uneasily next to Mr three-piece while we listened to a female voice from inside an office. Back in Mazomanie you'd never hear a dame swear, but whoever this broad was could dish out cuss words like a long-distance truck driver. The door came open and I waited to see the source of the bad mouthing – but she went in for one more go.

"And you can stick your f***ing clothes up your f***ing a**, they're not worth f***ing lifting anyway and if you think I'm coming back for your c*** a** f***ing fashion launch, you can f***ing k*** my f***ing b***er."

With that, she slammed the door grabbed me and, still angry, hissed at me.

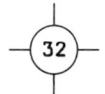

"Get me out of here – now!"

I escorted the lady back into the lift and out onto the street. Now I recognized her. Winova Traveller. She was a movie star, once, but was now in the running for Best Serial Shoplifter having starred mainly in evening news bulletins being strong-armed into a cop crate.

Once outside, seeing no paps around, she seemed in a better mood.

"Thanks pal. Where's the usual guy?" I told her I didn't have the Jones what was going on, but I was happy to help. I hailed a cab and we piled in.

"Christ!" she puffed in relief. "Sometimes I think it would be easier to pay for this stuff." She took out scarves, perfume and a neat watch from her pocket. She looked me up and down: "You go in there on the steal as well?" I explained what I thought had happened and how I'd have to go back later for some new rags."

"Hold on there, pal," she said, feeling around inside her coat sleeves. "I think these might fit you – and she pulled out a pair of black leather trousers." I took the strides and looked on amazed as she shoved both hands up her skirt and produced a Dolce and Gabbana gold T-shirt. "I'd have some socks for you too," she gasped. But they dropped out my bra when that bitch grabbed me.

She dropped me off and told me to try Sacks 5th Avenue in Bel Air – lifting stuff there was a cinch. I headed back to Benny's to get ready for my big night out. I squeezed into the leather pants and slid the T-shirt on. As long as I didn't breathe out in a hurry, I'd get by. That's if I even got past the bouncers at The Slam Bar. I rang Snarling.

## Chapter 5

"It's Schitt," I said, as he picked up.

"Maybe, but it's better than *America's Got Talent*. Who's this anyway?"

"It's Jack Schitt."

" Oh, hi Jack. Hey, you hear the kid fessed up? No need to go haring around town looking for assassins. Just a jealous guy, as the song goes."

I wondered what they'd done to the poor kid – waterboarding or threatened to call his mum.

"Mark. Know the Slam Bar off Hollywood Boulevard?"

"Know it? I part own it. Looking for a night out, Jack? Doesn't seem like your scene. Tony Bennett's on at the Staples – I could get you tickets if you want."

I was tempted. I began to hum "I left my heart in San Francisco" to myself. Then a picture of the dame's body interrupted the broadcast.

"Can you get me on the guest list at Slam?" I asked. "I wanna get a feel for these punks – where they hang out, what they get up to."

"Sure Jack. Just mention my name – don't embarrass me though."

He hung up. I checked the mirror. "Don't embarrass him!" He probably thought I'd go in my raincoat.

## Chapter 6: While the City Sleeps

The kids waiting to get into Slam looked like they had a good hour shivering in the cold, but there's something especially cool about walking straight past a long line all the way to the front. They all stared at me as I passed, probably wondering where they recognized me from. The goons on the door weren't exactly inviting. With puffer jackets and bad ass attitudes, it seemed surprising that anyone got into the club. One ran his eyes down my rags, sniffed and said: "Gay night tomorrow sweetheart." And looked away. There was a snigger from the front of the queue.

"I'm a friend of Mark Snarling. He's put me on the list."

"Oh yeah? Whassur name?"

"Schitt. With a 'ch'," he looked the kind who'd make something of it otherwise.

The goon ran his finger down the page on his clipboard.

"No shits here bro," he deadpanned. "None with a 'ch' anyway."

"He must have forgotten. I spoke to him an hour or two ago. Can you give him a ring?"

"Oh yeah, sure. Mr Snarling, there's some shit here trying to get

## Chapter 6

in the club? Shall I let him in. I don't think so – now take one!"

He jammed his hand against my shoulder. I wasn't in the mood. Jesus might have said turn the other cheek, but the good book never mentioned him being denied entry to the temple by a couple of Egyptian hoods. I swang round and went to sock him in the button. My fist hit a wall of white shirt that near turned my knuckles inside out, and, seconds later, a flying elbow attempted to ease my jawbone away from my face and I tumbled backwards down the stairs. I got up, rubbed my chin and looked back at the line. They were cheering.

Then I heard a squeal. "It's the detective." Just like an angel, but in a more revealing costume than Gabriel would probably allow, Jasmira came out of the darkness.

"You OK? Sorry I can't remember your name but follow me."

She sweet-talked Mr Iron Elbows and, avoiding eye-contact, I followed her into the club. We pushed our way through the crowded bar and up some steps.

"The VIP room" – she mouthed. "Stay close."

Another set of monkey men, all suits and smiles, stood patrolling the cordoned-off area. They unhooked the rope for Jasmira with a pleasant good evening and eyed the rest of us suspiciously as we hung on to her slip stream.

Inside was a little like O'Mallogons – in that they had a bar. The rest of it bore no comparison. The white leather sofas and crystal chandeliers were illuminated by blue and purple lighting. Projected onto the wall were famous iconic film clips mixed into an Andy Warhol-type two-colour palette. In the first couple of minutes I picked out *Gone with the Wind*, *Reservoir Dogs*, *Butch Cassidy* and *Turner and Hooch*. It was pure Hollywood excess and I felt pretty comfortable in it even if my leather trousers were producing strange noises when I rubbed against the sofas.

As a waitress in a black catsuit poured me a glass of Cristal, Jasmira came over, shouting in my ear above the hip hop that filled every cushioned corner of the room.

"What brings you here, Mr Detective?" her voice tickling my inner ear. "Apart from taking on the bouncers in a no-holds barred?" She smiled and I wondered if I could have ever had a daughter like that .

"I was meant to be meeting some friends," I lied – I still didn't know who to trust in this town – "but must have mixed up the time or place."

She introduced me to her friends – a bunch of smart, good-looking kids from UCLA. They didn't seem to mind having someone twice their age as company and we chatted about Jas's chances of winning the show. Most of them thought Melrose was going to win, but if she was knocked out then Jas was surely the best of the rest.

I frowned in puzzlement at Jas? "Knocked out?" Yep. She'd been knocked out alright. Blipped, bumped and blown down. Jas sidled over and did the shouty ear thing again.

"They don't know," she explained. "Snarling says the cops want it kept quiet. They're going to say she had to leave the show due to family bereavement."

Suddenly she grabbed my hand. "Come and have a dance," she bawled as she pulled me up. Slowly my trousers un-bonded with the sofa and I was led down onto the dance floor. Now I'm about as a good a dancer as Michael Jackson was at plastering, but after a couple of glasses of Cristal I fancied I could shuffle around and throw my arms in the air as good as the next 40-something.

It was all cupcakes but I wasn't getting under the skin of this jive house. Snarling part-owned the place and Jas comes here but

## Chapter 6

probably so do the rest of the show's cast and crew. If I was on the look out for someone with a big sticker saying "Melrose's Killer", I was going to have to look a little harder. I went to the John. Not that I thought I'd find anyone there. I needed to point Percy at the porcelain.

"Hey, Jack!" I heard a voice whisper. I couldn't tell who it was and I couldn't turn round mid-pee. I stretched my eyes round as far as I could, but only succeeded in getting my brogues wet. I finished up and looked round. "Come here, Jack," a voice came from the small crack of an open cubicle door. It was one of Jas's uni friends. I took a step towards it. "Best wash your hands first." Jesus, they were well brought up kids.

The boy was smiling. Maybe he had the info on the rub-out.

"Fancy doing a Hyundai?" He offered me a light green tablet with a picture of Elmer J. Fudd printed on the top. I looked the kid in the eye?

"Drugs?"

"Sorry, sherriff," he said, closing his hand pronto. "I just thought you ..." He suddenly looked pretty uncomfortable.

I thought quickly, my brain fogged by the glasses of bubble. I've got to get into this scene like the old-time ops with their reefers and the jujus. If Marlowe was a 21st-century Dick what would he do?

"Sure kid." I stuck my flat palm out. And he hesitatingly dropped the baby. "Thanks," I muttered, trying to swallow. I went to the basin for some water.

Back in the club I took another glass and eased into an armchair. I watched the scene as I waited for the junk to kick in. Nothing happened. The kid had probably been duped with some harmless candy. The club was filling up and a big group had taken over the VIP area. They were loud and confident, even among the young and pretty brigade that was there already.

I watched for a while then pushed my way in. I found a tall, shaven-haired fop in a red suit and gave him a big smile.

"You look great," I told him. He nodded back and I felt a rush of affection towards him. "Fantastic suit," I continued and suddenly I was in full flow. "Isn't this place fabulous, look at those lights – blue, green, red, blue again, wow. Have you had a drink? That Cristal is nectar man. Get some down you. You should get down on that dance floor – it's bangin' brother, I don't know where the tunes are coming from but they're rocking the joint. And the John – you seen the John? I reckon they're real diamonds on the shitter."

Red and his mates were staring at me – in amusement and slight disbelief as the leather-trousered stranger knocking on 50 carried on spouting bollocks ten-to-the-dozen. Eventually I checked myself. I loved these guys but there were so many people here to talk to.

"Watch the Es though guys. I think they're fakealoo." I proceeded to hug each of them and told them all I'd love them forever before going back to Jas and the others on the dance floor.

"You met Venice Budgetlodge and her gang then?" she shouted as I jumped up and down, screaming and punching the air with both fists. "Oh yeah, they're great guys," I answered. I thought maybe I might ask her to marry me, when the song finished. For a second I thought, did she say Venice was here? Then the thought went as Jeremih's "Birthday Sex"came on – what a wicked track!

How many hours I spent shaking everything I'd got, I couldn't rightly tell. I jumped, twisted, shimmied and sweated like a pig in a sauna. My Dolce was dripping and under the leather I'd developed a nappy rash that would put a six-week baby to shame. I finally sat

## Chapter 6

down. I had a thirst that could empty the Hoover Dam. I took the whole bottle of Cristal and took a long draft. I caught sight of Jas as she worked her beautiful ass through the crowd. Christ, she was special. I couldn't tear my peepers away from her.

I watched as a couple of people from the big group went over to her – two guys and a flame-haired dame. It was Venice. I felt warm for Jas, she really was on the up with friends like that. Venice could really help her.

I carried on watching them, trying to focus on what Venice was saying. It took me a while to realize she wasn't giving vocal tuition – she was tearing a strip off of my girl with her two thugs looking on menacingly. I hurried up the stairs and pushed my way to her.

More of her rubes saw me coming and closed up, stopping me getting to her.

"Jas, you OK there?" I called. I tried again to push through, but the muscle wasn't letting me past.

"Come on guys," I tried pleading. "Can't you feel the love in here tonight?" That's when I felt the first punch sink into my belly so hard I thought it would come out the other side.

I felt the T-shirt rip as I was picked up by my collar and thrown mug-first at the fire escape double doors. My shoulders hit the door bar forcing it open and as I tried to get to my feet I was kicked down the first flight of stairs. Getting roughed up is an occupational hazard for a private dick; we all work out our own means of dealing with it. "Please don't hit me," I pleaded. "I have a rare blood-type." They kicked me around and threw me down another flight of stairs. "Watch it. I'm a friend of Steve Wilkos." I lost count of the blows. I hit the pavement. Hard. I looked up to see the queue still tailing back around the corner. They were cheering.

## Chapter 7: Where the Sidewalk Ends

```
I woke up with a hangover. This time it was
a bad one - the men with the jackhammers had
started on my temple and didn't look like
they were due a break any time soon. Someone
seemed to have scraped the fluff from under the
wardrobe and spread it on my tongue. That's
the last time I drink Cristal, I thought
to myself. Then, slowly, the events of the
evening came back to me. I'd been taken out by
Venice's gooks. Why would they do that? Because
she didn't want strangers getting too close?
Because they knew I was a dick on a case? Or
maybe they just didn't like my D&G shirt?
```

When I finally screwed my eyes open I had another surprise. I wasn't at Benny's. Not unless he'd brought in painters and decorators and worked on those stains on the carpet while I was asleep. I was on a couch in someone's front room. I staggered to my feet. My legs waved the white flag and I sank back down, wincing with pain. Across the room a figure came running in through the open French windows.

"Jack, don't get up. You need to rest darling. I'm just taking a shower, won't be long." It was Jasmira, looking even more

## Chapter 7

gorgeous in her dressing gown. No make-up and her hair still falling over her face. She sure was some ankle. She explained how her friends had helped bring me back here. Venice's stormtroopers had played volleyball with my head until someone had spiked me through the doors and out of play.

I watched through misty eyes as she slipped into the bathroom. She left the door open and I could hear the water crashing against the opaque glass of the shower cubicle. I stretched my neck a bit. It hurt, but I could just catch sight of her arm and the silhouette of the side of her body. I shuffled towards the end of the couch pushing my shoulder against the armrest. Jas was lathering up. I closed my eyes. My groin still ached with the imprint of a size 11 boot from last night; it really wasn't ready for any stretching exercises. But if I moved a little more I could still catch her as she emerged from the cubicle. I fell off the sofa.

It took me ten minutes or so to climb back into position, every bone in my body begging to be left alone. Jas came back in combing out her half-wet hair.

"What was all that about with you and Venice last night?" I asked. "She was giving you such a hard time, I thought I'd come and help."

"Oh, that's just Venice. She was a bit high – started accusing me of stealing from her house when we went for a shoot last week."

"Stealing what?"

"I wasn't sure – she was just ranting about putting her reputation on the line for us and this is how we respond."

"Some reputation."

"Listen honey, I've got to go. Make yourself comfortable and

I'll see you late. Ciao!"

And she was gone. I drifted back to sleep with the memory of the cutie in the shower still imprinted on my mind. I slept for hours. Pictures filled my head of goons landing punches, of laughing Mexicans, of a dead girl in a blue dress – anything but Jas in the buff. What did a man have to do to get a decent dream around here?

I was woken by the phone. I couldn't tell where it was but I recognized the voice as soon as he started leaving a message.

"Are you there? We need to talk. You've got to think this over, baby." The tone was pleading, all Snarling's arrogance wiped away in a sorrowful whine. "Don't pack your bags now, when it could be so great. Call me – please!"

Things seemed to be going awry for Goldenballs. First his best girl is found dead, now the new favourite is thinking of leaving. He's not going to have much of a show left at this rate. But why would she leave when she had so much to gain? Was it just the pressure? Were the threats to the competitors getting heavy? Or maybe the bust-up with Venice had something to do with it?

Every which way I looked at it, things were getting heavy. And I was in the middle of a rainstorm without an umbrella. The kind of umbrella that got people to talk – and listen. If the Chicago lightning started and I had no shooter, I'd be caught like Snow White at a wicked Stepmothers' convention. This thing had gone past the watershed and if I was going to stay up with the big boys, I was going to have to put my pyjamas on and brush my teeth.

LA is the city of the smoking gun and yet I had no idea where I'd get one. Back home I could go to Honest Mart, Bob Getcha

## Chapter 7

(anything) or Dave. Dave didn't have a good epithet, but he usually came up trumps. Here, I could hardly look in the yellow pages. Well I could, there were hundreds of gun stores – this is the USA, where every god-fearing sap and his granny carries a Glock – but none that would sell one to me. The Second Amendment might insist on "the right of the People to keep and bear arms" but they don't include people who have accidently shot the wiener dog seller at a Mazomanie football game.

Then I remembered what my mother had said: "Didn't I know it's easier to buy a gun than an apple in South Central". But where was South Central and how did I get there? I grabbed the paperback guide *Get To Know LA* off Jas's desk. South Central didn't seem to have a lot in the way of tourist attractions. But it merited a brief paragraph warning of gangs, drugs, poverty, crime and drive-by shootings. It sounded just the place for an op man on vacation.

Burned-out cars, boarded-up shops, litter-ridden streets – this was my part of town. The people walked with heads hidden in hoods or necks buried in shoulders; they looked away when they saw you coming or crossed the street to avoid making contact. These were my kind of people – fruit of the earth, who when they trusted you would take a pellet to save your life.

I smiled at a lad sitting on the front step of his block. He flashed his teeth at me. "Scram, white boy," he snarled. "You feel me?"

A couple of blocks further on a group of young kids were hanging around the corner. They huddled together passing something in their hands. With a smile, I remembered my young days swapping baseball cards and how serious we would get about it.

"Hi gang, anyone got Ramirez?" They stared at me.

"No Ramirez? What about, er ... Jeter? A Griffey?"

"You po-liss?" one of them asked

"Am I what?"

"Po-liss, 5-0, cops?"

I was now wondering whether a phrasebook would have been handier than the guide book.

"We don't got no Ramirez or Jeters," the leader, who must have been all of 12, said.

"Any of your mums or dads around?" I asked, changing the subject and looking around. It didn't go down any better than my baseball card gambit.

"You in the game, mister? You civilian or a fiend, mister?" the leader demanded. "You want Red Tops? Blue Tops? Milllies, Phillies, or Hamsters?" I wasn't sure what their game was – maybe a kind of hide and seek by the way his friend kept looking up and down the street – but I had no time. I strolled on, there must be somewhere here I could get me a shooter.

"So long kids. Enjoy the game." I looked at my watch. "Mind you, you should all be getting back to school pretty soon." As I turned the corner half a brick flew past my ear. Kids today, eh?

I must have walked the streets for hours, but all I saw were kids on every corner playing the same game. It could have been spring break. But it was looking like I was on a pretty fruitless op and I was destined be the first dick in LA not to carry metal. Still aching from the beating, I turned my heels and headed back

## Chapter 7

towards the subway station.

"Sssss," a sound I can't make through my front teeth echoed from an alley as I passed. I looked in past the old cardboard boxes and big drum trash cans. In the shadows I half saw a figure.

"You the cat talking to the hoppers?" he asked.

"Shoppers?" I was getting a bit sick of the slang. I'd only just got up to speed on my gangster spiel.

"Hoppers? The kids?"

"Listen, tough guy, I'm just looking to make a deal." The last thing I needed was more trouble. He beckoned me to follow and led me into a derelict house. On the ground floor, two hopped-up guys lay on the floor. We went up a flight of stairs and he was joined by three or four busters – all with scarves pulled up over their faces. I was pushed into a room while my guide and the others waited outside.

A well-dressed dude in a suit I couldn't afford sat at a desk, like some Wall Street bean-counter working on his portfolio.

"Excuse my crew, brother." He sounded like the only projects he'd seen were on his law course at Harvard. "We have to take care of security."

I nodded. "The po-liss."

"No. They're cool. It's the others."

I nodded again. "Crips and Bloods?"

He shook his head. "The Docks."

I hadn't heard of them but I nodded anyway.

"You said you wanted a deal? How big a package, Bro? Ten kilos?"

Was he talking drugs? I couldn't be sure. "I'm looking for a lead slinger." Now he looked confused. It was time one of us gave in and talked English. "A gun?"

"You got the cheese?"

I nodded and tapped my wallet pocket.

He opened a cupboard. "Uzi? A Klashi? An Aki?"

"I was hoping for someone a little more personal – I'm not looking to take the whole town out."

We settled on a Beretta 21mm. It took a large bite out of my Snarling cash but I figured he might be good for a few more bundles of Hamiltons yet. I handed over a wad and pocketed the Roscoe. It felt snug, right. I was comfortable at last – like when I'd finally got my racoon pyjama case back after my mum put it in the wash. I was about to shake the dude's hand when a chill crept over me.

There's always a moment before it all goes off, when I know it's going to happen. It's a sixth sense, but as metaphysical skills go it's worse than useless. It comes so late – there's no time to do anything – a bit like when you see the dog crap a second before your foot is in it.

I heard panic and shouting and looked at my man. He looked scared. "It's the Docks," he squealed and we dashed out the room and headed down the back stairs. Taking three stairs at a time, I really felt I could get away. I saw the light of a ground floor window and made for it. Then I heard a crack, was blinded by a flash of light and inevitably I hit the ground.

The sudden complete silence was shocking. For two seconds I really thought I was in heaven. The light was now brighter than ever. Then I heard voices, one of them faintly familiar.

"And, action!"

## Chapter 7

"Just another day's work in South Central for the ruthless teams who own these streets. These guys, who don't seem to want to talk to me, belong to one of the most vicious gangs in the world. This week on *Dave Camp's Gangs*, I'm going into their world."

"Cut!" shouted the chick with the clapperboard, slamming it shut with that gunfire sound again. And the lighting guy turned off the heavenly glow.

"Great," said the guy who had been doing the talking. "Now, let's get out of here – I think I've had an accident." A small wet patch at his crotch was growing bigger by the second.

"Oh not again!" she sighed. Then she saw me. While her guy trembled, looking down the street in a state of panic, she took me aside. They were working on an English documentary series on the toughest gangs in the world. Dave Camp, the spineless chicken in the corner had been chosen to present the series on the basis of playing a tough guy, Martin Hard, in over five series of the TV soap *Walchurch Square*. She was at her wits end.

"He called in a helicopter to get him out of Moscow, wouldn't get out the car in Ruanda, shat himself in Hong Kong and paid for a body double to film his part in Columbia. I've only got him out of the hotel room here by promising I'll get him backstage at the Liza Minnelli concert tonight. The series will be a disaster if we can't get hold of Elijah."

The sound of spilling dustbins interrupted her rant. We looked up to see the gang leader who'd coughed up my bean-shooter scrambling away.

"That's him!" she shouted and gave chase, closely followed by the lighting man.

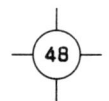

"Don't leave me on my own!" cried Dave Camp, reluctantly joining us.

Out of interest I joined the chase. Elijah was desperate, but they, and I, wouldn't give up – following him over scrubland, scaling wire fences, darting across a four-lane highway and eventually into a disused factory.

"I'll wait here," said Dave.

The building was dark and all we could hear were occasional footsteps. I followed the TV guys in. Could it be a trap? Did I really need to be here? I reached into my coat and gripped my Beretta. Somewhere in the building I could hear low voices. We gradually tracked them down to a room at the far side. As we stood outside the room, I looked at the producer and she cautiously nodded. I gave the door a sharp kick and it fell open.

In the corner Elijah stood in the light looking confused and scared. In front of him a camera crew and interviewer posed. A woman in headphones turned round.

"NBC – *Darren Does Gangs*, we got him first, suckers."

## Chapter 8: Farewell, My Lovely

```
I woke up to the sound of a reggae band with
the bass turned up to max. They were playing
somewhere between my cranium and frontal lobes.
The TV producer had been a big drinker. I can't
remember much after my second ginger beer but
I'm pretty sure she had got me home. I ran for
the pile of clothes on the floor and, relieved,
retrieved the roscoe from my pocket.
```

My cell rang. It was one of these new screen ones, and I really hadn't fingered how to use it yet. I pressed some words on the screen.

"Hello? Hello?" Nothing. Then came a voice as smooth as honey with a silk ribbon on top.

"Hi. It's Venice here."

"Hi," I answered as cooly as I could. But she couldn't hear me – she was just leaving a message. Damned phone.

"Apparently some of my friends didn't offer you such a warm welcome to LA the other night. I'm very sorry – they were only trying to protect me but they can go a bit too far sometimes. I'd like to apologize, personally – see if I can't make it up to you. Give me a call. 6555-4000 and not a lot of people get that (she added with a giggle) – Tooda-loo."

Sure her monkeys had roughed me up a little. But coming over all Betty Boop? To her I was Mr Nobody from Nowheresville, she hardly needed to keep me sweet. Still it was useful to have her number; she was on my list for a little call and response. I'd leave her to stew. Whatever it was she was worried I was going to do, it would do no harm for her to carry on fretting.

I headed back up to the studios. It was rehearsal time for the competitors. By the time I got there they were in full flow. As they ran through an Elton John medley they all looked pretty friendly to me. The rivalry had been fiercer in the Mazomanie Carnival Queen case (yours truly had been detailed to dig some dirt on the 19-year-old favourite and, somehow, those implant surgeon's notes had reached the *Trumpet*).

But there was one noticeable absence from the rehearsal. No Jas. Had she left the series already? As soon as he'd finished murdering "Don't Let the Sun Go Down on Me", I tackled Marko.

"She got called in to see Snarling," he explained. "That boy's got it bad for her. She's playing him hook and line and good on her, man." It was a sweet deduction but I realized I was the only one who knew Snarling was piling it on thick because his biggest talent was thinking of packing it in.

I hung around for the rest of the rehearsals. These kids were having a ball, they were helping one another out and were generally so nice they made the von Trapps look like the Manson Family. If someone was tilting the pinball machine, I was pretty sure it was none of the singing and dancing Waltons in front of me.

Eventually Jas came back. Either she was heavily allergic

## Chapter 8

to her mascara or she'd been bawling like a baby with a dirty diaper. She grabbed her bag and went to leave. The others tried to remind her that she still had to run through "I'm Still Standing" but she ignored them, turned on her heels and headed for civilian drive. I tried to catch her eye.

"Hey Jas, thanks for the.."

"Yeah sure."

Her mind was clearly somewhere nearer Alpha Centuri than Hollywood. In just a short time, I'd grown attached to the broad. She'd picked me out the gutter twice the other night and seemed like a swell dame. I followed her out.

"Don't quit Jas," I called.

She stopped and looked quizzically at me.

"I heard Snarling's message at your flat, I..."

She tried to smile. "You've got it wrong, Jack. Not now, OK." And she left.

I headed outside and watched her stride across the car park. Hollywood, eh? Tantrums and tiaras. It was another scorching day and I was sweating under my hat and raincoat. It was a pity, there wasn't a summer outfit for a detective – but you'd never have caught Mick Hammer in a Hawaiian shirt and shorts. I checked my reflection in the side of one of the outside broadcast lorries filling up with gas. I might be sweating like a pig in a sauna but I looked the part. It was time. I took out my deck of Luckies and felt the thin roll of paper against my lower lip. I flicked my 50 cent Lakers lighter and got an inch-high flame. As I slowly inhaled, the end of the cigarette began to glow. I was there.

"Put it out!" The shout rang round the car park. I glanced up to see a security Joe rushing towards me. I took the loosey out of my mouth and looked where he was pointing. The sign said "Gas Station – inflammable liquid – Strictly No Smoking." For Christ's sake, I thought. It's health and safety gone mad. I flicked my butt.

"Noooooooo!!!!" Mr Uniform shouted as he turned and ran.

The hospital said I had only superficial burns and that my eyebrows would grow back in a month or so. But according to a doctor, who looked about 12, I was in shock and they wanted to keep me in overnight for observation. I told them that when I observed people I took a flask of coffee, some sandwiches and spent most of the day hiding in shop doorways and that they were welcome to follow suit. Besides Snarling was already going to be miffed about the cost of a new lorry, let alone settling my medical bill. Still, aching from the boot leather of Venice's goons and now with a bandage wrapped round my hat line, I eased myself out of bed. My phone rang and I fished it out of my trousers. I pressed every button I could see on the screen.

"Schitt, Schitt, Schitt" I repeated in case anyone could hear me. Somehow I struck lucky.

"Jack, it's Jas. I need to talk to you."

"Sure babe, fire away." This was going to be interesting.

"Not here. Meet me at the Bubble and Spin Washeteria in LaCrema Park at ten".

Like they always say, being a private dick is a dirty job. I'd been in LA just a few days but the grime, blood and burn marks on my cottons told their own tale. Seeing as I was heading for a launderette – though quite why she wanted to meet there I

## Chapter 8

couldn't fathom – it seemed too good an opportunity to miss. I headed back to Benny's. As usual, Benny was sat at the front desk in his vest watching the baseball on a small TV. I could have driven a herd of buffalo up the stairs and he wouldn't have noticed. I reached over, grabbed my key and headed up to my room.

It was gone. The small card I place in the door as I shut it had fallen to the ground. It was an old trick I learned from a James Bond film. Someone had gone in. I tried the door handle. It was unlocked. I grabbed the Beretta and pushed it open. The room looked different. Things had been moved. I heard a shuffling from the bathroom and walked towards it. I gently pushed the door open, trying to stop the roscoe shaking around in my trembling hand.

There was a scream. And a woman rushed out past me...

"Meu deus que você está fazendo! Coloque essa coisa que é perigoso você imbeci! Você é um lunático! Maria Mãe de Deus!" She left her cleaning trolley behind. Dammit, I thought. Didn't James Bond ever have maid service?

You get some funny looks when you're sitting on public transport with a New World grocery bag full of stinking clothes, but at least I had no worries getting a seat. LaCrema was out in West Hollywood, a good walk away from the Boulevard and the coffee shops I'd made my landmarks. This was respectable family country, no place for an op scratching away at the city's underbelly. It was getting dark. Kids were being called in for their supper and the streetlights flickered into action to no obvious effect. I stopped a patrolling private security Jeff and asked him if he knew the Washeteria joint. He took a glance at my bag and sent me further into the maze of houses, roundabouts and play areas.

The Bubble and Spin Washeteria took its place next to a café, an organic veg shop and a bookshop in a row of one-storey buildings, purpose-built amenities for the residents. Its lights marked it out as the only one open at this hour. I pushed my way in and took a seat on the bench. Someone had made an effort. It was clean, brightly painted and smelt of bubbles. There were a couple of people busying away at the dryers but by time I'd packed my clothes into the washer they had all disappeared. I had a quick look out the door and, seeing no one around, I took off my trousers and gruds and packed them in the washer. Jas would be an hour yet, I could sit here in my raincoat with everything dangling free and no one would be any the wiser.

I bought my powder from the dispenser, fed the dimes into the machine and picked up a copy of *The Globe*. It didn't take long before my eyes rested on a photograph of Venice. I wondered what she'd done now – another sex scandal? A bitch-fight in a club? An academic paper on ontological dialectalism? Nope. Apparently she's split up with her longstanding boyfriend (three and a half weeks) and was looking to enjoy herself as a free agent. Hey, I smiled to myself. It looked like I'd picked a good time to visit her.

I watched through the window as my clothes danced hypnotic circles and, as the machine eventually stopped shaking, they collapsed in an exhausted pile. I grabbed a basket and took them over to the tumble dryers. It was nine-fifty. I had ten minutes to get them dry and get some kecks back on before Jas appeared. I fumbled for my change – I needed two 50 cent coins. I could have sworn I had at least three. I came up one short. Shit.

Ten minutes. I ran – in my socks, shoes and raincoat and nothing else – back in the direction of Wilshire. After a couple

## Chapter 8

of minutes I stopped for breath and saw the torch of the security patrolman. He had no change. He ran the light down to my bare legs, I shrugged and ran on, finally reaching an all-night drugstore and got my change. It was dead on nine.

My ameche went. Maybe it was her. Wrong. It was a dame I cared about but not at this moment. My mother. I told her I couldn't talk right now but she was one persistent woman. What was I doing there? Didn't I know it was easier to buy a gun than an apple in South Central? Then there was a long tale involving her friend Mrs Ormerod and her scabies. And how she hadn't seen the cat for three days. By the time I got her off the blower I was ten minutes late. She'd wait. Wouldn't she? I forced my aching limbs back to the Washeteria.

I pushed open the door. There was no one there. Great, I thought, there's still time to get my trousers dry before she comes. I fed the fiftys in and set the machine in motion. Knackered, I leaned back against the dryers, closed my eyes and tried to get my breath back. When I opened them the familiar rotund figure of LAPD's crack detective met my gaze.

"Officer Krupke?" I said, startled.

"Lieutenant Chzopski," he corrected me. He paused, then spat out, "Jack Schitt, I'm arresting you for homicide. You have the right to remain silent and take one helluva beating from an ugly 17-stone Irishman who is still pissed about the Dodgers moving; the right to an attorney if you're a chickenshit coward looking to plea bargain your way out and you have the right to spend the rest of your life at hotel state penitentiary, gratis – all meals included. Apart from that, your mine."

"Cut the crap, Chopsticks. What homicide? I've been here all night." He was going to have trouble pinning this one on me.

"Not a great alibi, Lee Harvey," he chuckled. "Cuff him boys."

As he moved I saw her. A mess of blood covered her face and most of the wall at the back of the launderette. I must have been in such a hurry when I'd come back, that I'd managed to miss a stiff with three pints of the red stuff over her. Good detective work, Schitt. Even after someone had let the daylight into her top end, she still looked beautiful to me. My eyes misted up and my heart pounded.

"Jas!" I screamed. But nothing came out. Chzopski gave me a look like I was something he'd scraped off his shoe. She'd been shot. Through the head. Point blank. And here I was the only person for miles, with a gun and no pants.

Chzopski's goons went to put the bracelets on. I put my hands in the air. They searched me and pretty quickly found the Beretta in my inside pocket.

"Got the weapon, Lieutenant!" the uniform shouted triumphantly.

"Way to go, McGarret," I applauded. "You'll make detective yet, son." He jerked my arm back. "Hey lieutenant! Can I just get my clothes?" I nodded to the dryer.

Chzopski didn't even look up. He had tilted his head and was looking at Jas as if she was a difficult putt on the 18th. "Crime scene evidence, Schitt. No can do," he muttered.

The bulls grabbed my sleeves and pulled me out past the security patrolman. He was still looking smug for having dropped the dime to the keystones.

"Filthy pervert," he snarled, glancing down at my bare legs.

They threw me into the car and we headed for the clubhouse.

## Chapter 9: You Play the Red and the Black Comes Up

```
I woke to the sound of doors slamming against
my cerebellum and reverberating shouts filling
my cranial ventricles. I made a mental note; I
really did have to cut down on the Red Bull and
sodas.  I lifted up my head and discovered that
this time the slamming and the shouts were for
real. I hadn't touched a drop last night. I was
laid out like a stiff in a mortuary on a wooden
bed with a pillow the size of a handkerchief
in a twelve by six cell. Over on the other
side of the pen, a jerk snored his way through
the whole shebang, competing - and winning -
against the noise of the cops bringing in the
daylight.
```

The image of Jas's map, with enough holes to make a colander, came back to me like a sledgehammer in the gut. Someone had got to the broad and worse, she'd been zotzed on my watch. Whoever it was must have plugged her while I was out searching for change. Who could have known she was there? Why would anyone bump her off? No wonder I'd got the pinch from Chzopski – he had no one else. Now he had me, and that seemed to be one step further than I'd got. And, he still had my pants.

## You Play the Red and the Black Comes Up

I'd made a statement to the bozos who brought me in last night. I told them everything. Well nearly everything. I left out the message Snarling left at Jas's apartment and the state she'd been in when she'd left rehearsals. Private investigator rule number one: always got to keep a little back for yourself. But I couldn't deny that I'd gone to the launderette to meet her – or that I'd been too busy attending to my smalls to notice her face had been rearranged with the help of some metal messages.

Meanwhile Mr Snorey was beginning to wake. He seemed in an even worse way than me – groaning and muttering to himself. I had a good glom at the Joe – did I recognize him? He clocked me.

"Had a good look, Blue?"

"Blue?" Was he a Cockney or maybe Scotch?

"What d'you have to use for a dunnee round here?"

I nodded at the bucket.

"Fair dinkum," he said, apparently in a better mood. He took a long pee in the pail.

The cell door opened and a buzzer looked in. He ignored me but threw a paper at Dinkum with some venom. He whistled through his teeth, shook his head and said, "There you go – Mr Gabshite – see you at the Oscars – I don't think!"

Gabshite? I look at him again and I remembered who he was. Mal Gabshite, the Australian actor. He'd been in loads of stuff from all-action, post-apocalyptic adventures to his famous role as a young homicide cop who hated his partner so much he went on to do 43 sequels with him. More recently he'd gone all Catholic. He'd produced a four-and-a-half hour dramatization of the Sermon on the Mount. It seemed kinda strange to see him in the

## Chapter 9

cooler. I stretched a bit to see what was so interesting about the news rag the uniform had thrown in.

"Mad Mal in Drunken Auburn Abuse."

"Christ on a bike!" he spat. Tossing the paper aside.

He fingered his cross and sulked like a baby. I went and picked up the paper. It turned out that Mal had been picked up for drunken driving the evening before. The unfortunate cop had a crop of ginger hair. Mal had enquired "if the cuffs and the collars matched?" and then had gone off on one about how red-haired people had been responsible for all the ills in the world – "Lucille Ball, Geri Halliwell, Ron Weasley, Mick Fu'ing Hucknall, that English prince, Diana or whatever his name is – you people are everywhere," he is reported to have shouted.

Usually this kind of thing might have been overlooked but Mal had been producing a six-part series for ABC called *Carrot Heads Are People Too* about the long history of anti-ginger prejudice. Now the whole series was in jeopardy. Many of the major players in Hollywood were copper-tops, sensitive about their image and the age-old prejudice about their vulnerability to sunburn and sharp tempers.

The tank door opened again and a young journalist came in. Mal brightened up. Holding his cross, he explained how sorry he was, how Jesus had probably been ginger and how out of character this was and it was all down to some pills he taken for his hay fever.

"She was a fu'ing Duracell too. I bet she dyed it," he snapped after she'd left.

"Hey dude," he turned to me. "What's the difference between a ginga and a terrorist?"

I shrugged.

"Well, you can negotiate with a terrorist!"


Eventually Lieutenant Chzopski appeared. He didn't look like he'd crawled out from under his rock on the right side this morning.

"Get up, Schitt," he barked.

Mal Gabshite began to get to his feet.

I waved him back down, "I think he means me."

I followed Chzopski's enormous backside down the corridor and into an interrogation room. There were two chairs, a table and a tape machine. Chzopski dumped a bag of doughnuts on the table.

"Hungry?"

I nodded.

"Too bad, Schitt. These are mine. You can get your own when you get out of here – which will be in about 15 years." He began stuffing them, one by one, into his oversized mush.

"What about my pants?" I asked. My thighs had been chafing. I wondered which amendment of the constitution gave a man a right to be questioned in his jockeys.

"Still at the lab," he spat back. "Fibres. We could find tiny specs of the deceased's hair or clothes on them. You never seen *Houston: Forensic Unit?*"

"Considering I spent the night at her box, it wouldn't be surprising." I countered. Chzopski raised an eyebrow.

"I never had you down as her type, Schitt?"

"Come on. I hardly knew the broad. I slept on the couch. We

## Chapter 9

were just friends." I took a deep breath. "Listen Chzopski, you know I didn't squirt the metal. I was just looking to help the bim. She'd asked me to meet her there, I don't know why?"

"Look at it from my direction, Schitt. You're new in town; the first time I meet you you're interfering with a strangled murder victim, then strike me down if you aren't loading the dryer while your 'friend' swims in her own blood in the corner, her soul already well on the road to St Peter's gaff. It don't look good."

I had to admit it didn't. People had sat on the fryer for less. But I had a cast-iron alibi for the first, and they knew it wasn't my gat that plugged Jasira. But I had no more idea than Fat Freddy here, who would want to blip off the two songbirds.

Chzopski was in full flow. "I mean. You could just be the patsy who does the dirty work. Maybe the clean-up man for some Hong Kong betting operation? Met up with a ruthless Triad gang lately, Jack?"

"Yeah. You got me," I smirked at the lieutenant. "I got chop suey from the Bamboo Express in Chinatown and got my instructions in a fortune cookie."

Chzopski got up. He was just out the door when he turned back to me.

"You a jockey's man or Y-fronts?" he asked.

I'd seen this on *Colombo*. They wait until you're off your guard and then swing the key question at you. I thought for a second but still couldn't see the significance.

"Jockeys, I like the room," I finally answered.

"I'll get the officer here to get you some," he mumbled as he left. "Christ. Horatio Caine never has to interview a man with his Johnson hanging out!"

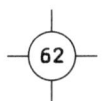

### You Play the Red and the Black Comes Up

I looked down. My coat had parted like the Red Sea revealing an arid land...

Back in the cooler, Mal Gabshite – pretty much like his career – had gone. I had some time. Just me and my head jelly. What could Jas have wanted to talk to me about? Did it have anything to do with her tears at the studio? Or maybe the bust-up with Venice? I couldn't help but think that Snarling might be a little disappointed in me. If he'd hired me to babysit his little darlings, the fact that there were now two less of them might cause him some distress. I needed to get out and do some gumshoeing, but the small matter of a bolted metal door and a lack of jocks made it a little difficult.

It wasn't long before my guardian angel settled both scores. The guard let in Snarling. He was carrying a fresh pair of pants in one hand and a bail slip in the other.

"That's 25,000 bucks, Schitt. You better not be involved in this – I want to see that money again. And look at the state of you – you look like some dirty old flasher."

"Nice to see you too, Snarling." I struggled to get the underpants on without taking my raincoat off. He looked away.

"Listen, Schitt. Maybe this was a bad idea. I'm sorry but you're out of your depth here. I'll put you on a flight back to Mazomanie tonight. You can go back to sniffing around dustbins and playing peeping Tom on errant husbands – no more rough stuff, no more lorries on fire, murders or losing your underwear."

"No way, Pedro!" I looked him in the eye. "I'm in it up to my neck now Snarling and I've got a hunch about whose pulling the

## Chapter 9

strings."

"That so, Jim Rockford? Have you told Hopscotch out there?"

"I just need me a little time, Snarling – I've got leads. I just need to tighten some screws and I'll get wise."

"Yeah, right. See you at the final then – with all of my babies still alive, if that isn't too tall an order for you?"

He threw a roll of notes at me and walked off humming the theme to *Murder She Wrote*.

Coming down those clubhouse steps, I felt like Nelson Mandela. You don't really appreciate your liberty until it's taken from you. I can't recall if the great man was ever incarcerated without underpants but after 13 hours at Hotel LAPD, I finally breathed the sweet air of freedom and felt the support of a double cotton gusset.

It had taken me over an hour to help the ox-heads finish their paper work but it was all worth it when they handed me back my heater. I told the schmuck it was a tool of the trade and he passed it over – to a Joe still officially on a murder charge! Maybe the police entrance test has got harder and they have to do colouring-in now as well.

I made my way back over to Jas's place. Just to see what the rumble was. I hadn't noticed what a well-heeled area it was when I came before – even the cats were wearing Prada collars. I sauntered along the other side of the street. Apart from the odd passing car there was no one. If the keystones had been, they'd skedaddled again and left the place quiet.

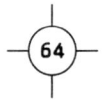

Her apartment was on the ground floor. I rang the bell, just to check there was no one there, and had a peek in through the front windows. The curtains were pulled and all I could see was part of the couch I'd slept on. Remembering the French windows and patio, I climbed over the side fence and made my way around the back.

A private dick has one great advantage over the feds – he doesn't have to obey the law. Well as long as he doesn't get caught. Chzopski would have had to fill in 14 forms to get permission to do what I was about to do in ten seconds: break into a dead number's gaff. Cracking open French windows was a cinch, especially if you been doing it since you were six. I wedged my key into the crack just above the lock. A quick jam with my palm and... the key broke in two. Another way was to ease the door open with your knee. I leant against the frame and gently increased the pressure on the door. Then half a key fell out the crack. Losing patience I grabbed a trash can and threw it through the window. See. Easy, when you know how.

I climbed in and pulled the curtains behind me. Chzopski had already been here – there was a Dippin' Donuts bag on the floor – so I wasn't going to find anything obvious. If only I could find a diary, a half-written letter to her mum or a tape where she'd spelled the whole story out, I could crack the case and open an office in Silverlake. But I couldn't.

I sat down on the couch and stared at the switched-off TV. I must be missing something. She was a good-looking twist – where was the love interest. Snarling? Too much of a slimeball. One of the guys on the show? She cared too much about her career. Maybe it was a pre-fame flame from home? Or maybe she was a dyke – Venice?

My cell phone played the two-note alert that I thought meant I got a message. I dug it out and looked. Nothing. Then it went

## Chapter 9

again. But it wasn't my cell. I dug down the side of the sofa and found a slim pink cell phone. Crackerjack! My thoughts raced ahead – contacts, texts, answerphone messages, my job here was virtually done. I stuffed the phone into my pocket and headed for the broken window. I'd got one leg through when I saw the car pull up outside and a figure get out and head for the house.

I climbed back in and stood behind the curtains. If it was Chzopski, I'd have some explaining to do. It wasn't. It was a skirt. A small, slim bim with a headscarf and shades on. She let herself in with a key and looked around. I heard her start to open each drawer in the bureau in turn. I peered around the side of the curtain to get a better look and, for just a split second, we seemed to stare each other in the face. I'd seen enough. I eased myself out of the window and lammed off – with a hefty clue in my pocket and a familiar face etched into my mind.

All the way back to Benny's, I felt the pink phone burning in my pocket. Everything was getting pretty goofy and I was getting a little paranoid so I let it burn until I was safely back in my room with the door as locked as it was ever going to be. I sat on the bed and put the cell in the palm of my hand.

It was an old-style phone – so much easier to manage than mine. As soon as I pressed a key, the text that had come through earlier popped up. It was a picture. Hard to make out exactly what – a sword with a snake wrapped round it – and the word "NIGHTS AMPIO."

I enlarged the picture and soon realized that it was a picture of a tattoo. Then I realized exactly where the tattoo was. I dropped the cell. The dirty bugger! "Jeez, that musta hurt," I sighed. But why send it to her? Did that constitute some kind of threat? I wondered. Or a promise.

I had a look at the rest of the calls she'd received. All were text messages from the same number over the last month or so, all had pretty awful spelling. They started out with "I dreemd bout u last nite – got v exsitid." And increased in intimacy until, whoever it was, was promising her something he knew she was looking forward to. Judging by the photo that followed, it wasn't a pair of Manolo Blahnik boots. For her part, Jas didn't seemed to have used the phone – either that or she had carefully deleted her sent messages.

I put the cell phone down and picked up my own. There was a call I still had to make. Carefully I punched in the numbers I had scribbled on the desk. It rang three times.

"Hiya?"

"It's Jack," I announced, "the detective you got your friends to beat up?"

"Oh no," she giggled. "They were just playing. If I'd set them on you, you'd still be trying to retrieve your phone from where they'd put it. I'm sorry we never got to say hello properly."

Oh but we did, I thought. Tonight.

"Maybe we can put that right, Ms Budgetlodge," I was back in op mode. "I could do with asking you a few questions – mind if we meet up, say tomorrow."

"That'll be cool. 4.00pm OK for you, Mr Detective? 1102 Pacific View Drive, up in the hills."

I muttered my assent.

"Tooda-loo," she panted.

I raised my eyebrows to the heavens.

# Chapter 10: The Female of the Species

```
I woke with a hangover. World War Three
had broken out between the two sides of my
brain and my mouth felt like the inside of
an Armenian taxi driver's glove. I must have
really got myself pretty smoked last night
after I spoke to Venice. Next time I'd go easy
on the dandelion and burdock.
```

It was time I got myself a crate, so I headed off to Jimmy's Rentos. Jimmy chewed the hind off a cigar while he showed me a chevvy with the sides caved in; a mustang with a hole in the soft top that looked like someone had gone through it in an ejector seat and a Camaro that only shot on three cylinders. In the end I plumped for a beat-up 1993 Ford that'd been around the clock.

Those Hollywood hills can take it out of an economy class rent-a-wreck and even by the time we reached the Canyon, the old girl was wheezing like an asthmatic on a winter cross-country run. A few miles up the winding road, I ditched Jimmy's pride and joy and walked the last half-mile up to Venice Budgetlodge's hilltop penthouse.

Trudging up the 18 steps to the porch, I drew a final deep breath, made a mental note to get a bit fitter if I was to start smoking and rang the bell. Waiting for whatever lackey, friend or hanger-on would answer, I looked back down over Tinseltown.

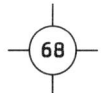

The view over the city was stunning – enough to give a retired realtor a stiffy.

Down there were four million people busy chasing a crock of shit at the end of a CGI rainbow. Innocent born-again boys acting in gay porn (and beginning to like it), still thinking George Lucas is about to call; Venezuelan cleaners desperately saving to send their hop-head, gun-slinging sons to a college they'll drop out of after two weeks; waiters, car valets, prostitutes, pushers... and somewhere, Jasmira's murderer. I struggled for a cliché to some it all up. "God, I love this town." I whispered. It was the wrong one, but it'll do for now.

As the door opened, I spun around to find an even more stunning sight. Venice herself – in figure-hugging white silk hot pants and a semi-transparent white sheer chemise.

"You must be the detective man – Mr err...?" she purred.

"Schitt." Was it really so difficult?

"Sorry – something wrong?"

"Jack Schitt? My eyes ran up and down her figure like an overcharged scanning machine.

"Of course. Well, put your tongue away Mr Schitt and come on in."

I followed her along the hallway – a trophy room of framed tabloid headlines, the little girl born with a silver spoon's journey to celeb stratosphere: "A Night in Venice", "Party Girl Venice Pulls Again", "Venice. Can Al Handle Her?", "Very Nice Venice! The It Girl Caught on Tape", "Sex, Drugs and the Cameras Roll", "Sex Vid Venice Runs Riot".

Then the blown-up photographs, all testaments to her conquests and excess: a worse-for wear Venice hugging Jack

## Chapter 10

Nicholson; a loved-up Venice staring into the eyes of Warren Beatty; giggling Venice rubbing the face of Hans Panter, lead singer of Jellignight, into the chasm of her cleavage; out-of-her-head Venice, surrounded by A-listers, dancing on a table in elite LA club Wild Horses; and a possibly sober Venice in a suit, shaking hands with JK Rowling. I paused at the last. Intrigued.

"Receiving my children's literature award," she announced by way of explanation. "Surely you've heard of my Chastity and her Pony bestsellers? I wrote them all myself – well the titles anyway, except the ones they changed."

"I hadn't – any other hidden talents I should know about?" I replied, looking her full in the eye. Oh my, this was cunning. I could be referring to her obvious achievements in the pirated sex videos that had oh so cruelly been put on the web or just maybe her ability to murder a young girl in a launderette in plain view.

"I'm pretty mean with a saxophone – it's a mouth thing." And she gave me that look. The one that sent a 1000-volt charge through my groin and sucked my buttocks in with the force of an industrial compressor. My cunning seemed to have legged it out through my still gaping mouth.

With a shimmy she led the way into a lounge. A well-known animal lover, Venice had made the decor a tribute to nearly every endangered species on the planet. A leopard-skin rug, tiger skin sofa, elephant feet stalls and snakeskin lampshade – all it needed was a Blue Whale pouf and a Panda Bear trophy head on the wall.

"Do you like to drink, Jack Schitt?" she asked as she bent over the drinks cabinet, her pretty little cheeks stretching to get out of those tight pants.

"I'd prefer a Jack Daniels." I got that one in quick and smiled to myself. Actually, I hated the stuff, it went straight to my head, but the line sounded good. Naturally I blew it pretty quickly: "on the rocks, with some diet lemonade."

She brought the drinks and sat down next to me. Close. Too close. You'd have been lucky to squeeze a kipper between us – although that might have gone some way towards dampening the sexual tension.

"So how are you enjoying our naughty little town, Mr Big Shot Detective?" Her finger stroked her lips then began walking up my sleeve. The broad was getting to me, but the word "detective" brought me back to earth. I was here on a business, with no perks – not even luncheon vouchers.

"All silk – until some babe gets doobed while I'm giving my gruds a soaking. But listen doll, bumping gums is no use to me right now; I didn't come up here on some trip for biscuits."

"Sorry Jack, I didn't understand a word of that," she murmurred. By now, her tongue was tickling my ear and I was regretting that decision to go another day without using the nasal and ear hair trimmer I'd picked up at the airport. Not that Miss Tabloid Filler 2010 seemed to care.

"I need to bend your ear..." – it suddenly seemed an unsuitable turn of phrase as her tongue had now curled its way around my lobe and was knocking it around like a contender in the boxing gym – "...about Jasmira D'Neeve."

"Oh that poor sweet girl," she squealed, suddenly switching from porn pussy cat to caring aunt. "She had such a bright future, and now, now..." She paused to wipe a non-existent tear from her eye. The dame had slept with the greatest acting talent

## Chapter 10

in the world but their acting skills seemed to be one thing she hadn't caught from them.

"I'd been working on media technique with her, how to handle interviews, pose for the paps, red carpet etiquette..." Christ on a chopper, now it seemed I was sitting snugly next to Professor Pussy, world expert in Tabloid Theory. I had to butt in.

"I've seen your work babe. That was some ing-bing that you frails had at the clip-joint."

She looked puzzled – for a second I thought I'd rung her number. Then it hit me – she hadn't grasped the vocab. How long had she lived in this town?

"The row at that club? Slammer?"

"Oh sweetie," she smiled patronisingly. "All staged. She hadn't been in the tabloids for ages, two or three days. Five minutes screaming at each other and the next day it's front page "Venice Bawls out Jasmira" and she's back in the limelight. She was pretty grateful, the poor little angel."

Was she for real or just taking me for a palooka? The doll had sure looked upset. I took another gulp of Tennessee Jack's cordial and felt for my box of butts. It seemed a great time to start my career as a smoker – light up like I really mean business. I reached for my bikini girl lighter – the one where she undresses as you flick the flame – in my suddenly too tight trouser pocket. You only get a few seconds before it looks like you're playing with yourself and I'd lost my chance – she was looking at me as if I was already waving it around like a roscoe.

"If that thing's loaded, I'd hate for it to go off now," she pouted in mock seriousness. "You might be needing it soon."

I decided to take up smoking tomorrow.

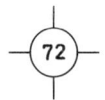

## The Female of the Species

I struggled to think what else I had to ask her but the effects of the JD, the tight pants, the tongue and the array of dead animals were disconcerting. I loosened my tie and attempted to concentrate.

"Did you ever go to her pad?" I asked as the room slowly began to spin.

"Oh no, the students only ever came here... Are you OK sweetie? You seem a little confused."

I felt I just needed a little air. I got to my feet and struggled to stand steady.

"Maybe, you're not used to the drink," she said putting an arm around me and guiding me out of the room. "Come and have a lie down for a minute, you'll feel better for a rest."

She led me down the corridor and up the stairs.

"We call this the studio," she says. "Make yourself comfortable detective and we'll see if we can't make you feel a whole lot better."

She pushed me and I fell back onto the bed. It was huge, with soft black satin sheets that engulfed me as I fell into it. Behind me a selection of whips and handcuffs hung from the walls. Venice knelt down between my legs and began to undress me. I looked up and watched the scene unfolding in the mirrors that covered the ceiling. Was there really a beautiful twist, half my age, making love to me in some kind of sex chamber? If so, how come I wasn't enjoying it?

My eyes opened. I was naked. I'm not sure how long I'd been out, but I'd sure had some weird dreams. Then I had another thought, maybe they weren't dreams. I felt exhausted but sketchily recalled a naked Venice in my arms; Venice

## Chapter 10

manoeuvring me skilfully around the bed; Venice moaning "Yes! Yes! Yeeess!" Suddenly, another figure entered my memories – a man! I scavenged my brain to try to reveal what happened next. All I could come up with was him saying, "Can you not get him a bit more... you know?", "Take fifteen..." and "That's a wrap – thanks everyone!"

I looked around the room. It was empty apart from my clothes, folded neatly in a pile by the door. The ceiling mirror, no longer played out a fantasy from the back of my mind, but reflected an out-of-shape ageing man. Now I realized that in my earlier rapture, I'd missed the coup-de-grace of the room – a selection of cameras, presumably remotely operated from another room.

I got myself dressed and walked back downstairs. Now I'd thought of a few more questions for the heiress with the lairest (OK, that one didn't work). But all I could find was the housemaid and a note: "Thanks Jack, must do it again some time! Tooda-loo - V."

The housemaid explained that Venice had left over an hour ago and shooed me out the door. I walked back to the car trying to piece the whole shebang together. Venice must have passed me a Mickey Finn in the snort, got me into bed and filmed it. But I was pretty sure that, in the state I was in, I wouldn't have given much of a stand-up performance.

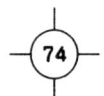

I'd become quite a regular at Bamboo Express and was on my way out to collect the Phad Thai they had waiting for me every night at nine. At the reception Benny and a couple of his friends were cackling as they watched something on their laptop. As I came down the stairs, he looked up.

"Hey, stud! You never told me you porno man! She hot stuff, hombre!"

Another of his friends joined in, pointing to the screen. "How you do that, man? How you do that without breaking an arm?"

I leaned over to see what they were watching and saw an almost familiar scene. It was the room I'd spent the afternoon in, it was the bed I'd slept in, it was my clothes neatly folded in the corner, it was the legendary Venice Budgetlodge kneeling on the bed, naked – but was that really me underneath her? I really couldn't be sure.

Someone had dropped the DVD off for me earlier, but Benny and his mates had been curious, ripped it open and to general amusement played it on a laptop. I grabbed the envelope and checked the compliment slip.

In scribbled words it said: "Hope you enjoy the film, Jack – you're quite a star!"

I twigged what she'd done. She was one devious broad. I was damaged goods, compromised. I'd bought the grift for the full ten dollars. Whatever evidence I might bring to the case regarding Venice would now be discounted. What a sucker!

## Chapter 11: A Man Named Dead

```
I woke up inside the snare drum of an angry
rock drummer. At least it felt like it - and
it was time for his solo. A couple of hours
shooting pool and drinking had left me a
century light and with a mother of a hangover.
I'd certainly racked up enough of those
alcohol-free beers to last a lifetime. I made a
mental to stick below 0.03% in future.
```

I checked in to see Snarling. I needed to know if he had a Chinese angle on the murders, some idea of who might have put the curse on his young singers. Snarling was busy but called me in anyway. He introduced me to Danny Bendham, a limey soccer player who'd come to LA to play his sissy-boy game. I took his limp hand and expressed surprise he'd bother coming to a land where no one gave a flying turd about his dumb-ass sport.

He smiled and said, "Well, I've got a few other interests here as well." He spoke with a voice so thin and weedy, I checked to see there wasn't an eight year old standing next to him.

Snarling butted in. "Euston Bendham?" he proffered, like he was expecting me to get out my mat and start praying.

I shrugged.

"The singer? Used to sing with The Zest Sisters? Twelve

number ones? She's been judging on the show."

I nodded, trying to get the conversation moved on. "Oh yeah, She's great." I needed this Brit ball-kicker out the way so I could chew the cud with Captain Smarmball.

"Jack's a good friend of mine from way back," lied Snarling. "We're doing a bit of catching up."

"Aren't we just," I agreed.

Apparently, so Snarling told me when he'd left, Bendham and his Frail were celebrity gold over in Britland and had come to LA like the rest of them – for a sprinkle of stardust. He was intent on mincing around on catwalks and she was thrusting her size minus two body onto every TV show she could.

"That's all sweet potatoes, Snarling, but let's start spitting out some hardball." Jesus, I was getting good at this, even I didn't know what I was talking about now! For a second, Snarling looked worried, then he smiled.

"Shoot, Jack. What's on your mind?"

"Why was Jas going to leave the show?"

Snarling played the innocent. I didn't have time for acting lessons.

"I heard your message at her box. The 'don't go' baby stuff. Real tear-jerker stuff, Snarling."

He looked relieved. "Oh that. Yeah, she was upset. It had all got a bit much for her – the competition, the press – she was under a lot of pressure, Jack."

"That it? None of the Jeffs putting the screws on her? No Jocko breaking her pump? No trouble boys running the jump on her?

"Come on Jack. This isn't 1954. She was stressed out, what with DOA and his video. It was hard work.

## Chapter 11

Who's DOA?" It was a monicker I hadn't lugged before.

"He's a rapper. You know, the gangsta rap vibe – all guns and ho's and gold teeth. He'd got Jas in to sweeten up his homeboy attitudes – the sugar to his spice. He works down at Compton, keeping it real and all that."

"Will he talk to me?"

"Sure. Tell him I sent you. But go careful, Jack. They're the real deal, these guys. Don't always appreciate any meddling.

I did some digging on DOA before I left. He seemed like some powerful pug. He'd had a string of hit albums, won Grammies and the like but he was notorious for keeping it all too real. He'd come up from the street, did some drug dealing, did some time and somehow got into rapping. Rumours abounded that he wasn't shy of flinging the lead, but nothing had ever stuck. Hey boy, I thought to myself, join the club!

DOA was signed to Deuce Deuce Records. They were just about the hottest record company around. Their logo was a .22 (hence the deuce deuce) and that was the message you got from the lyrics of their hits. They were trigger men who loved their homies and their ho's but if you didn't show respect you'd get pumped. Nice.

I dragged the rento-wreck out to the Deuce Deuce record studios in Compton. It looked out of place among the Porches and Mercedes being guarded by some heavy looking goons. Who would have thought that belting out a few nursery rhymes could call in the cabbage like that? I was in the wrong game.

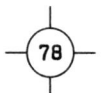

A group of young guys were sitting on the steps up to the studio. I could feel them watching me as I struggled to park the bang. As I got out of the car, one of them managed to tear himself away from the group laughing at my wheels. He hoisted his pants, and shouted down at me.

"You the Shit, man?"

I nodded. And he jerked his thumb backwards in the direction of the studio.

"Second office on the left."

I walked in through the glass doors past a life-size cardboard cut out of DOA with an Ouzi in one hand and a girl in pants that looked like they'd been sprayed on in the other. I reached the office. The sign on the door said "Daniel Oliver Andrews, Chief Executive, Deuce Deuce Records." Had I got the right place?

I knocked and a voice from inside shouted "Come!" All I could see was a copy of the *Wall Street Journal* sitting behind a desk.

"I'm looking for DOA – recording artist?"

"You the guy Snarling sent?"

"Uh huh."

He put the paper down. A young guy in his twenties, in dark glasses and a beret. He smiled and flashed a gold tooth at me. In front of him – on the desk – was a handgun.

I told him I wanted to find out more about Jasmira, that I was trying to get some idea of who could have chilled her off.

He carried on fixing me. I'd half expected this – these rappers have a language of their own – luckily, this time, I'd done a little research.

"Yo DOA. Jay a juice, yeah? Who'd want to get her murk man?"

He flashed the gold one again. This time with some words.

"I'm dreadfully sorry old chap. I understood you first time. I can't understand all that murk business though. Never have

## Chapter 11

mastered it."

"But you're DOA – the rapper, 'Dead On Arrival,' yeah?"

He smiled. There were more gold ones at the back. "Or Daniel Oliver Andrews, head honcho of Deuce Deuce – which one do you want?"

"Whichever can fill me in on Jasmira D'Neeve?" I gave back.

He laid his head to one side. "Aaah Jasmira. An awful waste of a life. She was a dream to work with; she had an absolutely splendid voice, could empathize with the essence of the lyrics straightaway – and didn't mind any of the sexist nonsense or all those dreadful guns."

Was I meant to swallow this bull? After all this was the man whose hits had included "She's Got Ouzi Suckin' Lips", "Ho Like the G in the B.O.O.tee" and "Old Shep", although that was a charity single.

I decided to plough on with my spiel. "Was there ever any Joes having around – keeping tabs on her?"

DOA laughed. "Mr Snarling wouldn't have tolerated that, Mr Schitt. He kept a very close eye on her. He'd often be down here himself watching her recording and he'd drive her straight back to Hollywood. He must be pretty distraught at losing that young lady. Would you like tea, Mr Schitt?"

While the boss made me a Lapsang Souchong, he continued to talk about Jas. He seemed pretty bemused as to who might have killed her and put it down to the awful crime figures in the city.

"There's just too many guns around, Mr Schitt. These boys grow up with no respect for human life and it's so easy for them to buy handguns, automatics, even machine guns. I've heard it's easier to purchase a gun than an apple in South Central –

although I'd never dare go there. It's a frightful situation."

I nodded at the piece lying on the table in front of him.

"This?" he laughed. "it's just a plastic replica." He tapped it on the table and tried to pull the trigger which wouldn't move. "I don't permit any firearms anyway around the building. Can't stand the things."

I'd had enough. "OK, D or Daniel or whatever you're called. Stop the flimflam and start talking straight. I've seen the videos, read the articles, heard you talking the gangsta talk, so cut the crap and the 'Mr Schitt's', put the Jap juice down and stop taking me for a palooka!"

He looked astonished. "I'm terribly sorry if I've upset you, Mr Schitt. You seem to be confusing my image as a singer with the real me. It's a business, a multi-million dollar business, detective, and I'm running a blue chip company. If all I have to read is a card written by one of my 'bros'," he broke off to smile, "then who am I to complain?"

"But what about the drug dealing? The time in the pen? The score settling?"

"Ah!" he smiled and waved his pointer in the air, "you've been reading Wikipedia. A work of genius, all fabricated, of course. I was brought up in Cape Cod, went to Harvard, you understand, studied Classics and Home Economics then did three years at business school – although I did have gap year working in a blind school in Indonesia."

There was a knock on the door.

"Are you ready boss? Nigel's on his way. He's got CNN this time."

"Great. Here you are Jack, this should be fun – the business in action. Nigel, or COD as we should call him, he does all the gun

## Chapter 11

and ho thing I do, getting almost as successful as me too! He's an old pal of mine from college. We've arranged this publicity stunt COD v DOA. Should be a hoot."

I followed DOA into reception.

"I say sweetheart," he asked the receptionist. "Did Two-Guns leave my notes with you."

The doll passed him some papers and DOA scanned through them.

"Excellent. I'd be lost without these. He's darn good though. Look at that?"

He pointed down to a line on the page that read: "Rise up, foo! You stupid mofo's got tough buckets or summin." Next to it was a translation describing how he was offering a fight and claiming his adversary had rather poor hearing.

A young lad came running up to me. He was sorry to have to ask me to move my rust-bucket down the street as it wasn't fitting with the image they wanted to convey on CNN. They really did think of everything.

In a screech of burning rubber, a dozen or so vehicles arrived outside the studio. They didn't bother with parking (just as well, as I'd discovered, it was a difficult space in which to manoeuvre) but left the limousine and various versions of Black Men's Wheels in the road. They poured out of the cars and assembled in front of the building. COD stood out front. He had a black suit over a black T-shirt, one chunky silver chain and a black cap pulled down over his eyes. He showed a silver tooth and called: "Hey DOA. You been dissin me bro? Yo big pussie man, come take some licks!"

DOA and his crew stood on the steps. I joined them. Reading off the notes pinned to a young guy's back, DOA shouted his reply.

"Fe bring it on, pouch," he turned to his boys. "Yo! I'm fixin to kill dis clown."

Suddenly all hell seemed to break loose. The gangs clamboured to get at each other and protect their man. Heaters were waved in the air and shots went off. DOA smiled at me: "Come on, Mr Schitt, lose a bit of that aggression. Let's hear your voice."

I began to shout and jostle with the rest of them and, as more shots rang out, I remembered the Beretta. I took it out of my pocket and waved it in the air shouting every obscene word I could remember.

Whether the safety was already off or whether I knocked it on someone's shoulder as I shook it in the air I'll never know. But somehow there was a crack that sounded different to the others and with a call of "He's been hit!" an almost immediate silence fell on the crowd and COD fell to the ground. My mind went back to the Hot Dog man in Mazomanie – surely history wasn't repeating itself?"

Within minutes the paramedics came and scooped him up. His crew disappeared as quickly as they had arrived.

As soon as the TV cameras had gone, DOA became a man possessed.

"I can't believe it, you shot Nigel, I mean COD. What on earth are you playing at?"

"I just got a bit excited," I said in my defence. "To be fair, I think I only winged him."

## Chapter 12: A Woman's Face

```
The evening news was full of the story. A -
thankfully fuzzy - unidentified white man was
circled in the footage as taking a shot through
the crowd at COD. It was Tupac and Biggie all
over again. Threats were issued and given back
by the lorry load. Every dust-up in the city
was said to be down to the DOA/COD feud that
was fast becoming a war. I needed a drink.
```

I headed for Poncho's Room on the Boulevard. I'd been told it was a space where a man could get quietly steamed with no one to bother him. In truth Poncho's was less a room and more a corridor with a bar running down the side. They had framed, signed photographs of the Hollywood stars who had graced the alley, presumably in days when people knew who they were. The photos were yellowing and the most recent was a smiling Sorrell Brooke, who'd actually signed it, "Boss Hogg". There were a few guys at the bar but the place was hardly jumping. I grabbed me a bourbon and 7 Up and took a stall.

The Dodgers were two up in the seventh, the Lakers were 90-70 in the third and Jack Schitt had zip with minutes left on the clock. Maybe Snarling was right. Maybe this wasn't the town for me after all. I'd been beaten up, played for a doozy, arrested without pants for totting a skirt half my age and I'd set off a rapper's war. I felt

## A Woman's Face

like the last man left in Loserville. I put my head in my hands, took a gulp and wondered if I could manage a whole glass of this stuff.

"Bad day, buddy?"

I glanced up through my fingers. The gee was in his late fifties, his bright red beezer clashed with his purple shirt that looked like it had a sample menu from a chop suey house splattered over it. All that was missing was a big badge with the word "Boozehound" pinned to his forehead.

I ignored him, but the Jeff wasn't taking no answer for an answer.

"Life is tough mister, that's the real deal." Behind my hands I winced as I knew it wasn't going to stop there. I was right.

"Thirty years on the force and out on my ear. There's your ticket now get the freak out of here, they said. No carriage clock, no long-service medal, no police pension, no card signed by goons who can't remember your name. It's a long walk down the clubhouse steps when you ain't never coming back, y'know?"

"I guess so," I mumbled, trying not to get a draft of his onion-and-beer breath. "That's a bad day fella. Too bad," I said as I tried to turn away but he tugged at my lapel.

"No not today – that was ten years ago. It still gets to me though. Every day."

I looked up at the sports again, still hoping he'd leave me alone. He stared at the screen too – nearly falling off his seat every now and then. The games ended. There was still half a glass of bourbon and 7 Up in front of me but the other half glass was already moving the furniture around my conk. I felt a little friendlier.

"What did they throw you for?"

"Huh?" He woke, surprised I was giving him the time of day.

"Why'd they fire you from the department?"

## Chapter 12

"Too much wheat and corn, Mister. Couldn't stay off the liquor. My partners carried me for a while, but they couldn't do it forever. They still look after me though – see I'm alright."

"Yeah?"

"I help them out on the odd moonlight job. When they think I won't trip over." He laughed.

"Did a job at her place the other day," He pointed up at the TV.

I was losing interest again. The boxing wasn't due to start for another hour and they were filling in with some cheap celebrity news show.

"Real sneaky like – in and out. Like the old days but this time I had no warrant. Swanky apartment though, up in the hills."

There was nothing as bad as old police tales – ever since I was a lad at O'Mallogans I been hearing their bragging and boasting. Most of it so much gumbo. I looked back up at the screen. A familiar face looked back at me. Venice. The sound was off, but I recognized the pout instantly.

Old red schnozzle was drifting off again but this time it was my turn to shake him.

"You broke in to Venice Budgetlodge's apartment?" I stared incredulously into his bloodshot eyeballs.

"Shhhh!!!" He put his finger to his mouth and looked round like the cartoon drunk he was.

"It wasn't so much breaking in as collecting – for a friend." He considered the matter dropped and returned to his scotch.

I pulled the drink away. "Hey pal!" he protested. I held the glass away from him.

"What were you collecting? Jewellery? Cash? Her dirty laundry?"

"Just a disc, pal. A CD, DVD or something. Now give me back

## A Woman's Face

my scotch."

I'd upset the old stoat. I wouldn't have many questions left. I called the bartender over and ordered another of what he was having.

"Can he take another one?" he asked, looking at the semi-conscious Joe.

"Don't worry. I'll hold it for him," I wisecracked back.

The new glass of corn brought his eyes vaguely back in my direction.

"Just one more question ol' timer," I gripped the drink and screwed him hard. "Who's the friend? Who got you to do the job?"

He smiled, took the glass, coughed and I waited. He shrugged emphatically. I took the glass back.

"I told you, I was just helping out. I never meet the fella. The guys called him Gorby – they said he had one of those blood tattoos."

I left him ten berries and the rest of my juice. I'd gone in a bum and come out a detective. How did that happen?

Back in my room I tried to piece what I had together. Was the missing disc the reason Venice was giving Jas the shake up in the club? Maybe even why she'd had her and Melrose pooped? It made me wonder what on earth she had to hide – it was pretty common knowledge that for a few greenies you could buy the "secret tapes" with her being serviced from every which way. Hadn't her God-fearing billionaire pappy even written her out of his will on account of her deviant ways?

Still, it was another piece to the jigsaw. Perhaps I should go out drinking more often. I kicked my shoes off and lay back on the bed. I felt like an op man again. I reached for the pack of butts on the bedside table, pulled a stick and lit up. I closed my eyes and took in the nicotine.

## Chapter 13: They Shoot Horses Don't They?

I woke with a start. I had a hangover. There was an incessant ringing in my head and my mouth and nose felt choked. And there was a beating on the door. Now, I thought, that is a new symptom. I dragged my head up and two things became immediately apparent. First, the door noise was Benny, running along the corridor, banging on every door shouting "Fire, fire – every one of you mofos out!" Second, the cigarette was lying on my chest, the red glow facing me. My shirt was smouldering, sending out a thin snake of smoke. I'd set off the fire alarm.

I checked the clock. I'd been asleep precisely three minutes. On the plus side, it seemed I didn't have a hangover after all.

In the morning I got a final warning from Benny. Any more rule-breaking and I was out. Getting kicked out of the worst creep joint in town would be the real pasta sauce – he'd let rooms to hookers, junkies, pimps and thieves, but some Joe lights a tar pencil and Benny's citing *The American Hotel and Motel Rule Book* like he was Billy Graham with the holy whatsit in his

## They Shoot Horses Don't They?

mitts. Maybe buying off the fire department wasn't as easy as scratching the LAPD's backs.

There was a note for me pinned to the wall by the front door. At least Benny and the Jets hadn't opened everything that came for me. It was from Snarling.

"Party at the Bentham's place tonight. I'll need you there to mind the kids – 7.00 at the studio. Don't embarrass me."

I checked my diary. It didn't appear that I had anything arranged for the next 20-odd years, so I could probably squeeze in a party mingling with the beautiful people. It wouldn't seem right to let the Bendhams down – they seemed such nice folk.

Down at one of the fit 'em and fleece 'em joints I hired myself a soup and fish for the night. An evening suit does something for a man. Gives him a self-confidence born of comfort and posture. So it said on their leaflet. Personally, I felt trussed up like a sack of potatoes, but I wasn't going to look out of place this time.

I took the flivver into the studio car park and parked next to Snarling's Lexus. He was already waiting by the car looking relaxed in a silk shirt and white slacks. He gave me the once over. I was concerned the Beretta was ruining the line of the jacket.

"Hey! It's James Bond," he cracked. "Where you been, Jack? No one around here's dressed like that since the eighties!"

"Go climb your thumb, Snarling. Are we going or just playing playground soldiers all night?"

"We just got to wait for Michael."

A tall, slightly overweight Jeff came ambling across the car park. In a bomber jacket and baseball cap he looked faintly ridiculous for a man his age – but I wasn't going to say that to his face – he looked like he could look after himself in a kick-off.

## Chapter 13

Snarling introduced me. Michael was Snarling's driver, bodyguard, enforcer, gofer – it seemed if the boss even took a dump, Michael would be there holding fragrant silk wipes.

"You'll two should get on," Snarling said as we sidled into the back seat. "Michael used to be a cop – LAPD."

"Jack here's a detective, Mike. You know – searching for clues and shit, not just pummelling some idiot until he confesses like you guys." They both laughed.

The short journey out to Beverly Hills shouldn't have taken long but Santa Monica Boul was eight-lane packed with the city's Saturday night crowd. Time for Snarling to get inquisitive. He wanted the rumble on who I thought had done for his girls. I couldn't carp – he was supplying the greenbacks – so I told him. Not everything. Enough to say that I had a hunch that a girl who had everything would always want a little more.

Snarling give me the slant. "Venice?" The name didn't seem to want to leave his lips. "She is kinda deranged, but why?"

"I'm working on that, coach." I said, staring out the window and smugly leaning back against the soft leather fittings.

We pulled into the Bendham's place around 15 minutes later. It was modest – for a Beverly Hills mansion – an Italian-style building with a fountain, swimming pool and two enormous palms leading down to a finely manicured garden. There must be some serious mazuma in this soccerball world – unless Euston was paying the bills.

It was a beautiful summer evening and the gardens were already well populated with Oscar de la Renta dresses and Hedi Slimane suits sipping cocktails. Sports stars, actors, politicians and singers – in fact anyone with a decent tan and an off-shore bank account seemed to be here. It was a *Hello* magazine editor's wet dream.

Snarling's protégées were all here and came rushing up to give their svengali a hug. It was a sudden whirlwind of teethy smiles, flashing cleavages and spiked-up hair. I hung around. This was what it was all about for them: glamour, luxury and as many roquefort-stuffed cherry tomatoes as they could eat. I started to earn my dough, checking they still had all their bodily parts and that none of them had faced a gun-totting heiress intent on rearranging their cute faces. When the photographer arrived, I joined Snarling's button, Michael, who looked uncomfortable in the evening sun, leaning against a pillar, taking in the scene.

"Nice work, eh?" It was a conversation opener – of sorts.

He looked at me like I'd farted at a funeral.

"A word to the wise, shithead," he said without even looking at me.

"My friends just call me Schitt," I said, trying to keep the charm offensive up.

"Butt out. Do your babysitting thing but cause Mr Snarling any trouble and your ass is mashed potato."

"And have a great evening yourself," I chirped back.

With that the goon took off his cap and pushed the sweat on his forehead back into his thinning hair. I flicked a glance and I couldn't miss it. A scarlet birthmark right across his front bumper – was that a map of India or an ice-cream cornet? I ripped my gaze away and wandered towards the stage where a small group had gathered.

"I wonder if I could just have your attention for a moment."

## Chapter 13

The sudden amplified voice cut through the low buzz of the assembled. It was a voice I recognized – thin, childlike and with an unshakeable tone of acute embarrassment. Danny Bendham.

The guy might have been coming to the end of his career as a soccerman but he still looked gave the impression of youth. His closely cropped hair seemed to accentuate his boyish looks and his white shirt made him look like he had just come out of school. Only the tattoos that spread out down his arms and up towards his throat belied the image. Then there was the voice. Had his balls ever actually dropped? His quaint English accent had been modified and now hovered somewhere between Dick van Dyck in *Mary Poppins* and Michael Jackson – lost forever over the Atlantic.

"I'd like to thank you all for coming and to get the party underway, introduce – well she needs no introduction – my beautiful and darling wife, Euston."

An explosion and a flash of smoke had me reaching for my gat, but it was just Euston emerging onto the stage. She looked extraordinary. Everything about her was slight, her skeleton looking desperate to escape – except for her huge globular breasts which sat immovable like mountains in a desert. As if to accentuate this she wore a tight, black leather cat suit, laced up at the sides with a huge V exposing most of her chest, her nipples looking like they were desperate for a peep at the open air.

Euston attempted a smile and went on to announce that, as a present, she wanted to give us a sneak preview of her new single. That was kind of her but I really would have been happier with something gift-wrapped – like some of the ice and oyster fruit she had falling off a chain round her neck.

## They Shoot Horses Don't They?

As I watched I couldn't get the image of Big Mike's map out of my mind – and the only other person I'd ever seen with a mark like that. The words of last night's hooch hombre ran past like a subtitle: "I never meet the fella. The guys called him Gorby." Gorby, the Russian guy with the splat on his noddle!

By now Euston had been joined on stage by two young black guys dressed all in white, while Danny, his two young kids holding his hands, looked on from the side. They squealed with excitement as she wrapped herself around her dancers, faked going cabeza with both of them and ran their heads down her exposed frontage. All the while, she was caterwauling something about "living the dream". No wonder Bendham looked constantly embarrassed.

I got a tap on the shoulder. I turned to find a face I knew well. I was more used to seeing him wielding a shooter, sweet-talking some kitten or putting the squeeze on some hatchet men – he was a lot smaller than he seemed in those flicks.

"Do you have anything macrobiotic?" he asked, politely enough.

What was I, the bionic man? I'd had a plate inserted when I broke my arm but I didn't think he meant that.

"Vegan? Lactose-free? Can you check with the kitchen for me?"

Then it clicked. The only other people dressed like me at the shindig were the waiters.

"No, no." I tried a disarming smile. "I'm a friend – a friend of Mark Snarling – I'm just er... overdressed."

"You could check anyway?" he stared me out. Then he laughed. "Only kidding."

## Chapter 13

"Stu, Stu Breeze and this is Julie," he said, offering one hand and gesturing to the broad beside him with the other. Of course, everyone knew who he was. A big shot actor who'd won more than a couple of those gold-plated statuettes – and now one of the heavyweight Hollywood producers. A recent magazine I saw had him listed as the number one most powerful celebrity in the world. Julie would be his wife – though you never really knew for sure out here – I'd never seen any of her films.

"She's pretty awesome, dontcha think?" he said, as he watched Euston writhe on the stage floor.

"I'm blown away," I agreed.

"We know Danny and Eust real well," he continued. "It's great she's got all that talent but she's a real deep spiritual person too."

"I can see that," I nodded as I watched her rub her groin against the mike stand yelping "Oh my God! Oh My God!"

"Not many people know," Stu confided. "But she's working her way through *The Road to Contentment*. On stage she was giving the impression that she'd nearly arrived.

Stu and his wife were leading lights in the Church of Ludicrology – a religion made up in The Sixties by the famous crime writer T Bone Slobbard as a joke, but since adopted by the Hollywood galaxy as their very own faith. They claimed that people had originated in eggs brought by little green men from the planet Zarg.

The religion had a complicated moral framework: for example, gardening, dentistry and board games – bad; wife-swapping and tax avoidance – good. Whether what you were doing could damn you or grant you eternal life could only be deduced by buying the book *The Road to Contentment* from T Bone himself (since his death – or "elevation" – available online from Slobbardindustries.com).

Ludicrology shared the concepts of many other religions: confession, guilt, belief, afterlife – but its USP was that it was exclusively for the very rich. There were no worries here about giving your money away or doling soup out to pond-life.

"And Danny? Is he interested in the book?" I asked, watching as the Brit looked on at his wife, for all the world like he was grinding his teeth into fine dust.

"Well..." and Stu smiled the smile that had women squirming in cinema seats the world over. "... he likes to look at the pictures. So many people are coming over to us now. Are you a spiritual person, Mr... er?"

"I only believe in three things," I told him "the banknote, the barroom and the..." Bugger, I couldn't think of another one beginning with b.

"The barrel of a gun?" he suggested. Bastard.

"Yeah, that'd be it."

Stu shook his head. "It sounds to me like you've got a stock problem." The Ludicrologists believed you needed to have a stock check of your life and address any problems before you can begin to be redeemed.

"We can sort that out, though. Luckily for you, I've got just the literature here," he said, reaching into his pocket. "Do you have your cheque book on you?"

A waitress came round and – while Stu was explaining that he couldn't take anything that had been anywhere near a black olive, "the devil's piles," – Danny Bendham himself arrived.

"Hope you're having fun fellas?" he squirmed.

## Chapter 13

"Great performance," I nodded towards the stage. "Euston's got a great..." I struggled for a second. "...a great vocal range."

"Yeah, she's so talented. She's designed her own lingerie range, made her own perfume, written a series of books about *Geri and Her Pony* – she really doesn't need to do the singing."

Yep. She could give us all a break I thought.

"And all I can do is kick a ball around," he added.

"I don't really know soccer," I explained. "Over here it's only played by women and children. Do they let straight people play in Europe?"

"Come and have a game and you'll find out – there's a celebrity match tomorrow."

"Sounds great." I said cheerily. I'd sooner have my fingernails pulled out one by one, I thought.

## Chapter 14: In A Lonely Place

```
As darkness fell, the party was in full swing.
I'd had a few cocktails and felt in the zone.
Through the crowd I caught Snarling's eye.
It was time for me to go pinch-hitting.
```

"Hey, Snarling!" I called. "Where's your friend, Gorby? Is he still here?"

I got the condescending half-smile: "I'd stick to Michael. The last person who called him Gorby to his face isn't back on solids yet. What d'you want him for?"

"He's got a DVD I was hoping to borrow."

Whatever Snarling's response, I had no time to react.

A flutter or excitement rippled around the crowd and a firecrackering of flashlights announced the arrival of more celebrity royalty. It was Venice Budgetlodge, the Queen of Sleaze. She'd out-dressed them all in a gold lamé dress and enormous stiletto heels, long enough to kebab a wild boar.

Venice seemed to know everyone at the party – maybe they'd all starred in triple x-rateds made in her studio. I kept out of her way but kept an eye on the bim as she worked the crowd. She was such a pro – air kisses flew, eyelids fluttered and fake smiles sparkled.

Then she got to Stephen, the Justin Timberlikey. He got the charm overkill. I recognized it from my time chez Budgetlodge. Venice could

## Chapter 14

really turn it on and off at the flick of a switch. He lapped it up as she latched those sparkling eyes on him and let her fingers walk across his body – getting more and more intimate. I kept watching and eventually they got up, grabbed a bottle of bubbly and headed inside.

She was as trustworthy as any skate-around Sally. I gave them ten minutes and wandered into the house, feeling my pocket to check the B was there. Upstairs I checked a couple of the bedrooms, kicking open the door but found neither a dead boy nor a couple dancing the horizontal mambo.

Finally, I heard voices: "There's nothing to be afraid of," Venice was whispering. "Just do as I ask and it won't hurt at all."

He seemed to be sobbing.

I put my heater in one hand and pushed against the door with the other. It swung open to reveal the couple on the bed. She rushed to put whatever she was brandishing back in her bag. He seemed shell-shocked. He got up, straightened out his diapers and skedaddled.

"Aah, Mr Schitt. You've come as a waiter? How beautifully ironic!" she said, as if someone walked in with a tin hand every time she got jimbly jambly.

"Your friend seems in a hurry to leave," I smirked.

"That's men for you," she replied. "No idea of romance."

"Yeah, ain't it funny how a .22 in your mush can destroy the moment.

She changed the subject. "How about you, Jack. Have you recovered from the excesses of the other day yet?" She enquired like we'd been for a ten-mile hike.

"Listen sister," I replied. "If I was capable of doing what was on that tape – I'd be down San Fernando getting good doowah for keeping wood and bumpin' uglies all day. That was a pretty elaborate ruse to pull, framing me up like a Ron Jeremy, just for a giggle with your girlfriends. Come on, Venice – what you hiding? You can share it with Uncle Jack."

"Hiding? I reckon you've seen every last sweet corner there is to see, Jack baby. I just needed some insurance – like they say, for life's little surprises. Don't be bitter babe, you never know, maybe there could be a sequel."

She did a little shimmy, her whole body loose under the dress and her tongue seemed to come out in slow motion and sweep across her lips. I felt as if she was licking cream off every part of my body. I thought back to the film of "us" and swallowed hard.

"I need to go to the restroom," I said.

I'd calmed down by time I reached the toilets that had been temporarily erected at the end of the garden. I perched over a urinal, averting my gaze as someone occupied the next space. As I stared at the wall, I remembered the image on Jas's phone. I allowed myself a glance at the Jeff next to me. Not him. Still, the urinals were an unexpected gift – it wasn't going to make my party swing but it was my hippocratic oath to follow every single line of enquiry. I dug Jas's phone out of my pocket and checked the picture – there wasn't going to be much mistaking that if it reared up beside me.

I revisited the restroom a dozen or more times over the next couple of hours. If anyone from the show, or people I'd seen them talking to, went to relieve themselves I'd amble in, take the next urinal in line and have a discreet once-over for any sign of a "NIGHTS AMPIO" tattoo. Blending in is part of a tec's trade. I never thought I'd have to do it in a gents' pisser but I reckoned I was making a decent enough fist of it. Now I'd just about given

## Chapter 14

up. I'd seen Cavaliers and Roundheads, Jack Kerouackers and Acorn Andys, Buster McThundersticks and Madeleine Albrights – but nothing resembling the member that I'd found on Jas's cell.

"No luck?" A tanned guy in a white suit and purple shirt open to the waist sat himself next to me. He was smoking a hay butt the size of one of Bugs Bunny's carrots. He passed me the hoochie and I took a draw.

"That's good shit," I rasped from the back of my throat. The guy gave me a warm smile as the smoke gradually came up again from my lungs, filled my mouth and carried on northwards. Johnny Juju was tickling the back of my throat, I spluttered and snorted, my eyes watered.

"It's pretty rich skunk, man. Take it all the way down, not too much," my new friend instructed.

I took another toke and smartened up my act. "I know you," I said, hogging his bo-bo. "You're, Fred Henry, that singer from Smash! I remember you and your pal, jumping up and down in tight shorts." I was already coasting from the weed. It was to be the last meaningful thing I'd say for a while.

He sighed, "Yeah, 20 years ago man – but I'm never going to be allowed to forget it."

"Really tight shorts though," I drawled. And I attempted a verse of their "Paradise Club" hit. "Great song," I nodded to him, "love that bit about the topless girls sunbathing!"

"Yeah man, well we all move on, don't we? Hey look, I saw what you were up to in there," he gestured towards the restroom; I obviously hadn't been as low key as I thought, "I think I can help you though." He got to his feet and beckoned me to follow.

I wasn't at my sharpest. The laughing grass had dulled my senses and turned me into a smiling puppy dog and I followed him without a murmur to his white BMW convertible. He revved up and sped up the drive leaving an arc of gravel behind in the car park.

By the time I stopped giggling a few minutes later, we had come to a halt by a park. The only light came from a building a few hundred yards from the road.

"You might find what you're looking for up there," said Fred pointing to the building.

I was confused. Did he know about the picture? I tried to work out what was going on but was too dizzy from the dope. So I just gave him a puzzled look, pointed to my own groin and said, "What, that?" He nodded. "It's where I come to find it." Now this really didn't make much sense.

We trekked up through the unlit park to the building. I don't know what I expected, but it wasn't a public convenience. "In there?" Fred nodded. I giggled. We went in. "First one's yours," he said. I tried to remember the picture and get back into private dick mode.

I don't know how long we waited, it seemed like forever, but finally a guy walked in. Fred nodded to me. Who was he? Why would I be interested? I wished I'd asked myself. Instead I stood there staring blankly as he went about his business. Except he didn't. He looked back at me.

"Like what you see, buddy?" He said with a smile.

I carried on staring and smiling and wobbling slightly in a circle.

"You want to come a little closer, buddy," he whispered. Did he have information for me? Was this how it worked in LA? We usually met in a coffee house or down by the river in Mazomonie. I took a step towards him.

He reared away and his tone changed immediately. "Right,

## Chapter 14

you're booked. Lewd behaviour – off we go, mac." No sooner had he put his percy away than a uniform came in. Together they cuffed me. He hadn't even washed his hands. As I was being led out, I caught Fred peeking out a cubicle door.

"What you been in then, sonny – *90210*? *Glee*? *House*?" The cop asked.

The other one joined in, "I don't recognize him, probably another one from some obscure Eighties English band!"

By the time we'd got back at the station and gone through the paperwork the effect of the weed was wearing off. The cops were pretty gentle on me – let me off with a warning. They'd taken the phone off me to check it out and surprisingly brought it back in one piece.

"He seems like a nice boy," the bull said throwing it back to me. "You should give him a chance instead of looking for strangers in Will Rogers Park."

Just as I was putting the cell phone back in my pocket, I heard the familiar rustle of a doughnut bag and the grating tones of one Lieutenant Chzopski:

"Can't stay away can you, Schitt? A social call? Or have you totalled another young girl while I've been having a dump?"

As the officers explained to him why I had been detained, he gawped and nodded at me.

"Fancy that, Schitt," he said, in between a gravelly laugh. "You're even more of a sleazeball than I ever imagined. And I'd imagined quite a lot." And he stuffed another doughnut in his chops and continued down the corridor.

## Chapter 15: The Big Knockover

```
It was sometime in the morning. I woke and
smelled the now familiar stench of Benny's
rotten carpets. I had a hangover. The kind of
hangover only wuwoos and champagne can buy. The
Great Escape was being remade inside my head.
The Cooler King was bouncing a baseball off my
scalp, a load of English guys were trying to
tunnel their way out of my ears with teaspoons
and somewhere deep within the skull, a prison
choir were singing at the top of their voices
to mask the noise.
```

Although I was no closer to putting the finger on Jas's killer, the previous night's work had not been in vain. I'd met Gorby, the man in possession of a DVD from Venice and I'd first-hand experience of the LAPD's entrapment and harassment of the city's cottagers.

Down in reception Benny was watching a football match. Mexico was playing some other country.

I tried to ingratiate myself with the man. "Is it the World Series?" I asked.

He flicked a glance and, ignoring me, looked back at the TV. I looked over his shoulders.

"Two points to zip. Hmmm," I observed.

## Chapter 15

"Skip off back to your pads and helmets, nancy yankee boy," he replied without taking his eyes off the screen.

"Hey. I'm a soccer fan too – heard of Danny Bendham?

Now he was a little more interested.

"Bendham. He was great for Manchelsea Knights. He's past it now though – those LA poseurs are all he's good for. You know him?"

"Uh-huh."

"Tell him to bring his wife round here – she's still got some use in her," Benny cackled and returned to the match.

I too stared at the screen – but I was lost in thought repeating the words "Manchelsea Knights".

I'd collected the Flivver from the studio and headed out for Pasadena where Danny Bendham's charity match was taking place. A couple of hundred had turned out to see him, a load of has-been soccerball players and some ageing rockstars have a kick-about. They hadn't started yet and I wondered if I could get a quick word in before they did.

How do you ask a guy if he has a tattoo on his Johnson? While I sucked on that one, a guy in a tracksuit came over and threw a bundle at me. I caught them and looked up at him.

"You got me jumbled up with some other boob, fella," I told him.

"Nah," he replied. "Danny said to give them you. The changing room's just over there."

I looked across the pitch. Danny was giving me the thumbs up. Great. I hadn't played soccer since third grade. I didn't even know how many points you got for a field goal. What would Marlowe have done? Told the dip where to shove his kit, probably. But Marlowe might have had a few more leads than me by now. I needed to earn some time with Bendham.

In the dressing room I pulled on the shirt – it was red with a big white star in the centre. The badge said "Hollywood Stars – Charity XI". The boots pinched a bit, but the rest of the uniform fitted pretty well. I trotted out onto the pitch. I told myself I'd run around for ten minutes and then call it a day.

"Hey Jack – where d'you play?" Danny called to me.

"At a clip joint usually – with a dodgy deck," I panted. Running onto the pitch had taken it out of me.

"Have a go in D," he pointed towards the goal.

"You forgot to give me any shoulder pads," I said as I turned.

I did pretty well for a while. I ran where they told me to. I stood next to Giacomo, an offense player on their team who they told me used to play for Italy. I smiled and said hello, but he was in professional sportsman mode. He ran past me with the ball a couple of times but one of my teammates assisted with a fumble and another intercepted. Mostly we had the ball because we had Danny at quarterback.

Then the guy playing cornerback rolled the ball out to me. It was the first time the ball had come anywhere near me. I looked up and saw Giacomo bearing down on me. I kicked it as hard as I could back to the guy between the sticks and just missed the goal.

"Corner," shouted Danny, "pick up your man."

I wasn't that stupid. I guessed what he meant. I went and stood next to Giacomo – real close and turned to wait for the ball to come back into the end zone. Giacomo stamped on my feet. Both feet at once. I fell screaming to the ground, but no one had noticed or cared. The ball flew across the goal straight to the

## Chapter 15

Italian goon who let it hit his head and fly into the goal.

Danny helped me up. "Still think it's a nancy boy's game?" he smiled.

I couldn't really walk for the rest of the game. I asked if I could go now, but they said "ten more minutes" so I stayed on, limping around. There could only have been minutes left when one of the opposing offensive players came flying forward with the ball. I was back near the goal and heard the cry from Danny – "Your man, have him Jack!"

I was a decent linebacker in my days at James Elroy High and I was transported back 30 years to a muddy field in Wisconsin. I limped as quickly as I could to towards the oncoming player and with a tackle coach Murray would have been proud of, put my shoulder into him and knocked him into touch.

Four or five players of both teams stood over him.

"Is he breathing yet?" asked one. Another called for the meat wagon. The Jeff seemed to have just been winded, but couldn't move his left arm or leg.

Danny turned to me. "That's 50,000 people you've pissed off, Jack," he said. "he's meant to be playing Hollywood Bowl tonight."

We finally filed off the pitch. I was still limping and now my shoulder was aching. I sidled up to Bendham.

"That was fun," I lied. "Listen Danny, I need a quiet wo..." I was interrupted by my teammates hoisting him onto their shoulders and carrying him back to the changing room.

For a man who had, the evening before, received a warning for lewd behaviour, staring at a famous soccer player's naked torso in the showers might not have been a great idea – but this was the job – and I wasn't about to get shy on the number. I made sure I stood next to Danny.

"Impressive tats, Dan," I remarked, real casual like. His body was like a canvas – there was a leaping tiger, some Japanese symbols, the names of his children and... I craned my neck to see.

He laughed. "Not many people know about that one. It's supposed to say "Knights – Champions 08", my team in England, we did the double... but you can't really read it unless... well y'know."

I nodded. "Or unless you had Jasmira D'Neeve's cell phone," I added.

He looked back at me – shocked and stunned – his yap wide open and the offending exhibit now partially obscured by soap bubbles.

An hour later, after he'd pressed palms and signed programmes, shirts and bodily parts, I sat in the passenger seat in his Lexus. He held his head in his hands and cried.

"Why did you do it, Danny?" I asked when the tears had subsided a little.

"It was just a little fun – well to begin with."

"Fun? Blasting a chick through a launderette wall?" I was going off the gee. Fast.

He looked at me, his eyes swimming in pools of tears.

"No. The sexting. The messages. Of course I didn't kill her – I hardly knew her."

I was no mouthpiece, but I knew enough to tell him that that wouldn't stand up in front of the man in the big chair. He wiped his eyes on the sleeves of his puffer jacket.

"You hardly knew her? Yeah? So why the big tears?" I grabbed him by the shoulders. "She just some other floozy to you, wasn't she?"

## Chapter 15

He sniffed big.

"If Euston finds out she'll kill me. Last time I woke up to find her with a pair of scissors and that look on her face. And then there's my career – look what happened to Tiger Woods."

"Keep talking soccerboy." I gave him the stare.

"I met her at the studio with Euston, we chatted a little and I liked her. Next time I saw her I gave her the phone. I kept texting but she never replied. Usually, they come back in an instant, we meet up and that's that. But not her. I called her, but she seemed terrified of Snarling finding out. I told her it was none of his business, he just ran the show, but she was scared."

He closed his eyes and carried on.

Then I had the idea of sending the picture – I was sure that would warm her up. Next thing I know she's on the news dead. But I didn't think anyone would trace the texts. No one knows about the tattoo – well not many."

"Yeah, well there's a new sleuth in town, gonzo – luckily for you."

"Luckily?"

"Yep. I got the phone..."

The sap held out his hand. I smiled, shook my head and got out the car. I shut the door without looking back. Unfortunately, the bruising on my feet where pizzaboy had jumped on me had swollen badly. I got back into the car.

"Would you mind giving me a lift back to my flivver? I asked, as he slumped on the wheel sobbing.

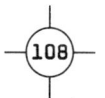

Back on the road I pulled into a drive-in for a burger and fries. That way I didn't have to walk anywhere. Could Danny have popped Jas? I doubted it, he didn't have the balls. He was a bigshot used to getting what he wanted – but there would always be other girls for him.

Back at Benny's I hauled myself up the stairs. My door was open but I'd long since stopped worrying.

"Maria!" I yelled.

I didn't know her name but guessed she could well be called Maria. She was probably cleaning the bathroom but I didn't want a scene like before.

The goon must have been waiting behind the door. I felt a blow to my head and I reached out to grab my bean-shooter. Before I could pull it out my jacket pocket I was thrown through the air and hit the bed. Nothing in there was well made. I felt the bed stand collapse under me and I sank back. He dived on top of me trying to grab the gun but feeling his body up against mine, I managed to let off a shot. It missed him. That seemed to make him even angrier. He pulled me up and threw me at the wardrobe. I hit it full on.

I tried another tack. "Can we talk about this?" I tried to say, but it didn't come out very clearly as he had his arm in my mouth. I felt the hairs against me teeth and bit down. It was partly successful – he took his arm out of my mouth but in what was clearly a safer option for him rammed his knee against my back. I rocked forward with a groan and he kicked me hard up the ass. That really was not in the detective-thug code of ethics, I thought, but didn't want to upset him any further.

He looked around the busted room and back at me. He took two steps towards me and said through his teeth, "The phone, punk." I took Jas's pink cell and flung it at him. Somehow I guessed I wouldn't get a thank you.

## Chapter 16: To Have and Have Not

```
So who had killed the talent show tucalalos?
I was beginning to care less and less. My feet
looked like calzones, one eye had closed up
altogether and, if I tried to sit down, it felt
like someone was pushing a jackhammer up my
poop-chute. I lay back on the broke-up bed. I
was beat. It was time to tear up my ticket and
get a regular pay check somewhere in civvyland
- something that didn't involve getting beaten
to a pulp every few days.
```

The phone rang. I tried to answer the damn thing but just succeeded in cutting it dead. A few seconds later it rang again. This time I managed to speed dial the Chinese resaturant. I hung up, waited a couple of seconds and sure enough it rang. Someone was pretty keen on talking to me. Through pure luck I managed to answer.

"Schitt!" I eventually barked.

"Detective Schitt – it's Roxy's mother – please we need you come here."

"I'm off the case. As from five minutes ago. Thank you." I hung up and went back to wondering if I'd ever be able to pass solids again.

It rang again. I answered – had I finally got the hang of the thing?

"Look lady, I told you..." I said in harsh, but what I'd like to think were fair, tones.

"But please, Mr Schitt. Roxy's been..." the caller took in air. "She's been..."

Oh Christ I thought. Not another one down on my watch.

"She's been really upset by someone."

What was I, some anti-bullying phone line?

"Yeah, well it happens to us all. Some Jeff hasn't made me too happy right now. Tell her to toughen up, that's showbiz, momma. If you can't stand the kitchen..." I forgot the rest.

"Someone's threatening her," She blurted out, "she got a message – in the mail – like a blackmail thing." The dame was pretty cut up. OK, her daughter has made the final of the show, but the two favourites had been already kaboomed, maybe she had good reason to be twitching like a rabbit.

"OK, I'll come over." The trouble with this job is you can't quit – not until it quits you. It wasn't the hat and flogger that made me a Dick; it was whatever ran through these veins (and was now splattered around the walls).

I dragged myself up and looked around the room. There wasn't a piece of furniture that wasn't smashed and light shone through the peepholes to the next room, where I'd squirted the metal. In many ways it was an improvement.

The show had booked Roxy and her mother a suite at the Palace Hotel in Beverley Hills: the same walls that Snarling had tried to get me to stay in before I chose the creaking pipes and roach-breeding luxuries of Benny's Downtown Hilton.

I took the elevator up to the 18$^{th}$ floor and Roxy's mother let me in to the room. It wasn't so different to mine – except it had a bed with springs, vases with flowers, a stocked mini bar and the

## Chapter 16

end of the toilet roll folded into a neat triangle – and a door that locked. I guess here, room service counted for more than being abused in ever more imaginative ways by the Jeffs in reception.

Roxy sat on the floor playing with her Barbies. Just like a normal ten-year-old. How cruel of the industry to portray her as the precocious star of the show whose knowing take on the gyrations and suggestive gestures of the elder performers suggested a sensual woman trapped in a child's body. Here her childish games mocked the sophistication with which she was portrayed.

Before I'd even taken my crown off, Mrs Roxy showed me the letter which had been left for them at reception last night. Just one sheet with letters cut out from a newsie:

"KEEP YOUR MOUTH SHUT OR YOU'RE FINISHED."

I wafted the paper in the air, there was something almost familiar about the scent but I couldn't place it. Maybe that had something to do with my sense of smell being handicapped by a smashed schnozzle.

"What's it about, Mr Schitt?" asked the mother. "What's she done to deserve this? She's only ten years old for heaven's sake."

"Can I speak to her, lady?" She nodded and said to Roxy: "The nice detective wants to have a few words with you sweetie, OK?" The kid put down her Barbies and looked up at me.

"Hi Roxy – I'm Uncle Jack, I just want talk for a minute? Maybe your friends can hang around and help if they want," I said, gesturing to the dolls. I was pretty good at this kindergarten spiel.

Roxy looked down at them and then back at me – "You don't think I really play with these do you? I've got a TV interview at 3.00 and my agent said to do the kiddie bit. I was just practising. And cut the uncle stuff, sounds like you're some kind of paedo."

It wasn't what I expected. I dropped the baby talk sharpish.

"Just a couple of questions then."

"If you've squared it with my agent." She sulkily pointed at her mother.

"She says you're upset about the letter."

"Too right," she snapped back. "She won't let me go to the press with it – that's headline Six O'Clock News stuff mister – I'm thinking of letting her go," motioning to her fretting parent.

I looked across at the mother. She nodded.

"Who'd do you think might send you this?" I dangled the letter in front of her.

Roxy shrugged.

"Could be anyone – I don't care who I upset, I'm going straight to the top. I want a number one album by the time I'm 11 and my own TV show after that."

I thought back to when I was ten. All I wanted was a GI Joe with a full complement of limbs (the dog had left mine a disabled war veteran suitable only for anti-Vietnam protest marches).

I persevered. "Have you upset anyone lately?"

She thought for a second.

"Well there's Dwayne T, Marko and Stephen – they're in the final with me so I have to bad mouth them. I slagged off Mark Snarling and Euston to the *Inquirer;* then I had a go at Britney, Lindsay, Millie – gee what a bunch of bitches – in *OK!*"

"Right. That's something to go on. We'll..."

"I haven't finished yet," she held her palm up to halt me. "I trashed Letterman on *Oprah* and Oprah on *Tonight* and both of them on *Disney Show Time*; I was mildly critical of the deficit control aspect of Obama's economic policy in the *Wall Street*

## Chapter 16

*Journal*, accused Sarah Palin of being a practising witch on *Fox.*"

"That it?" I said, giving up taking notes. She looked sheepish at last.

"And, er, I said we should bomb France at the United Nations."

I looked down at my list. One name stood out. She hadn't mentioned Venice. I checked.

"Oh no, she's been a complete angel, taught me all I know – I'm doing an interview on her later in the week. She showed me an advert 'Like a Mother to Me! – the other side of Venice' by Roxy Maguire exclusively in *LA Gazette*."

I left her to her Barbie rehearsal.

"She doesn't seem too flustered," I remarked to the mother.

"OK. I lied to you, Mr Schitt. She thinks it's part of the game. But I'm worried stiff – after those other girls got killed."

I tried to get Venice on the blower. It was time to get the juice straight from the fruit – but she was a tricky broad to lay the finger on. I left a few messages but gave up. I'd long been tucked up in the hammock when she finally called back.

"Hi Jack," she purred. "Looking for a chinwag then?"

I checked my watch – it was 2.20. Usually, it would be time for my nightly visit to whichever hellhole the dark recesses of my mind selected to torment me.

"I'm down at the Tiki Tiki Bar on Sunset," she said. "I could do with a little company, the no-rents I was with have all gone home.

I pulled on the least stinking of my clothes and rode a hack down to Sunset Boulevard. The Tiki Tiki was a tacky, '50s South Sea island-styled affair full of giant wooden carved people, stuffed parrots, palm trees and rattan furniture with the twangy sound of the Hawaiian steel guitar blasting out. I found Venice sitting on a barstool behind a mug as big as a vase.

"Hi Jack," she giggled. "Mai Tai," she said pointing at the mug. "It's just delicious. Fancy one?"

"I'm more of a Zombie man myself." The barman overheard me, I nodded at him and he went into action with the juice and the shaker.

Venice was dressed down in jeans and an "I Heart LA" T-shirt. This was off-duty Venice. A nicely steaming Venice. A different Venice from the one I'd previously encountered. I told myself to tread carefully. This broad was a human minefield – one false step and I could lose a metaphorical leg.

Though the lights were low, she soon caught sight of my rearranged facial features. She did a good act of being concerned.

"You poor baby, they must have given you such a pummelling. How many of them were there."

"A few," I muttered. "None of your doing was it, pussy cat?"

She adopted her offended look. "Why would I do that Jack? I've got you on a lead already, haven't I? But if you find out who did it just tell me and I'll..."

"You'll what?" I interrupted. "Cut up a paper and send an anonymous letter?"

She giggled and nodded. The drink had lowered her guard.

"Is that what you wanted to talk about? Little Miss Motormouth? Oh Jack – I thought you'd really got somewhere with this."

I took a gulp of my zombie – and felt my aching body begin to come alive, so I poured more down the gulch.

"That Roxy needs to shut up before someone shuts her up," she slurred, digging in her handbag. She pulled out a small lady-like pistol and aimed it at the imaginary child.

I took her hand and pushed it back down.

"For chrissakes Venice put it away – is that thing loaded?"

She winked at me and put it back in her bag.

"Jas, Stephen and now Roxy, what's your beef, pussy cat? What do they know?"

"It's nothing personal, Jack – they're good kids. Just TCoB – taking care of business. No one's going to wreck my career; I've worked too damn hard for that." She told me of a life lived in the public eye, of the pain she felt everyday of being disowned by her father and of her struggle to make it herself as a celebrity *sans* talent.

"You think it's easy getting in the tabs every week; the catfights, the dumb-ass boyfriends, pretending to like Britney and going to stay in Madonna's English stately home?" She finished her rant and stared at me.

"Enough to put the curse on them?" I asked, seeing out her stare.

"Voodoo? Hmmm I hadn't thought of that," she replied, a smile breaking out from ear to ear.

"You know blip them off, get them pooped." She still didn't get me. "OK. I mean have them killed f'christ's sake!"

Venice wasn't listening but was still staring.

"Hey baby, you still got blood round your eye."

She dabbed a tissue in her water and began to gently wipe around my eye. The gentle touch of her fingers took me by surprise and our eyes met. I felt the magnetic pull of her lips to mine and slowly leaned into her. The moisture of our lips met and gelled. Then I pulled back. Had she cleverly avoided the subject of zotzing the girls or was she really interested in me?

Either way I wasn't about to risk being taken for a palooka again.

Instead I talked. I told her of my own childhood in Mazomanie, how dad left when I was three, how dear ol' mom worked herself into the ground to bring up a family and how I finally achieved my dream of being a private investigator – a Dick with a ticket. I'm not sure how much of it she slept through, but she was slumped over the bar when I finally looked up. I finished my zombie, poured her into a cab and got another for myself. It'd been a long day.

## Chapter 17: Too Late For Tears

I had the mother of all hangovers. Forty clog dancers were performing "Riverdance" up and down my frontal lobes while a dentist drill quartet operated on my occipital. That must be why they called it a zombie.

I dug my best rags from the pile in the corner and attempted to look like a Dick who knew what was what at the bangtails. It was Finals day on the show and my last stint working for Snarling. I'd got no closer to finding Mel and Jas's killers and he'd made it clear the spinach was drying up. I was out on my ear once the show was over. But first I had to get through the show – that tightening knot in my guts was nothing to do with the Tom Yam Kung I'd eaten last night, but 30 years of prying, poking and eavesdropping telling me something unholy was going down.

Down at the studio there was a party atmosphere. The kids were out rehearsing for the show and the set was getting a fresh lick of paint for the occasion. I jumped the elevator to Snarling's office. Chzopski must have been at the doughnut shop when it opened; he was already in there chewing the cud with Big Bird.

"If it ain't Harvey Milk himself?" said Chzopski, as I entered the office.

"It was a stitch-up, Chzopski – just like the boy going down for bumping Mel," I answered.

I looked at Snarling. He shrugged.

"What?"

"Thanks Jack. You tried. I'm sure the lieutenant here is grateful for your help, but maybe there's a missing cat in Mazomanie that's just waiting for you to come back?"

I could've smacked his smugass grin all the way back to Wisconsin.

"You don't want me to finish the job? Check there's no funny business tonight?"

"Nope. Job done, Schitt," butted in Chzopski. "Well, job almost done – if you don't count two dead bodies and a busload of scared singers. Now do us all a favour and leave things to the pros."

"Take it easy, Jack," waved Snarling. He threw me a roll of cabbage. I picked it up and turned heels.

"Mind how you go now," chirped Chzopski as I left.

I went to read and write and got myself some java in a bar in La Brea. Snarling had taken me for a bunny, but I was still a Dick – just one without a sponsor. I had one last go at trying to crab what had gone on. Mel, the talented one had bit it in the dressing room; Jas, Snarling's favourite, had been chilled off just as she was going to leave the show; Venice was getting heavy with the stars one by one; and Snarling's man Gorby had had a disc lifted from her apartment. I stared down into my cup of Joe looking for an answer.

Instead, through the steam came the picture of Venice, miming with the shooters saying "Roxy needs to shut up before someone shuts her up," from last night. She was some goofy tomato and trouble had a habit of whipping down its pants whenever she was around. Would she do that to a kid? If she'd

## Chapter 17

chalked off the other two she surely could.

Outside, I took out a cigarette. I rolled it between my fingers and threw it away. I didn't need butts to prove I was a real detective – I needed to solve the case. I headed back to the studios. Snarling hadn't taken my pass and I flashed it at the chumps on the gate for the last time. I made my way up to the VIP gallery. Snarling would be too busy with the show to notice me, but I'd have to keep clear of Chzopski.

The area, perched above the rest of the audience, was packed and I had to squeeze my way to the front. I got there just in time to catch the guys finishing their moving tributes to their two dead competitors before rocking into their opening number, a real corny version of Hot Chocolate's "Every 1's A Winner".

Each one of them then went through a big production number, they got the audience to their feet and even the coolnote stiffs in the gallery were bopping up and down. I scanned the place for Venice – she made it her business never to be hard to spot, but couldn't fix my peepers on her anywhere. Had she given me the breeze? I felt a ripple of fear run through me. Could I be too late?

I counted my former charges, relieved as they all appeared back on stage – and with them came Miss Glad Rags herself – all hugs and smiles like they were her own von Trapp family. We were then treated to Venice telling us how much she loved each and every one of them and how she couldn't wait to hear their final songs.

First up was Roxy. She laid on the syrup by the bucketful, the audience lapping it up. I'd seen enough. I pushed and squeezed my way back through the crowd until, eventually, I was spewed out into the ante room. I looked up at the TV high in the corner where Roxy was milking her applause. What did I think? That Venice was really going to top the kid in front of 60 million viewers. I was a bigger klutz than they said.

I wandered down the stairs and into reception. The place was empty except for the blonde on the desk. I ask her to call me a cab back to Benny's. I took a seat and sat with my head in my hands. Through my fingers I saw Roxy herself, rushing down to the dressing room area. She paused to wave at the receptionist and ran on. I figured she must be down for a quick costume change.

Blondie waved at me to signal the hack was waiting and I shuffled towards the revolving doors. It was a slight movement but enough to catch my eye. In the reflection of the window, I saw a pink dress disappearing along the same corridor. Venice?

"Five minutes," I shouted at the cab driver, "I've forgotten something." It was gonna be more than five minutes but I figured he'd forgive me when he read the morning papers. I went back into the building and down the corridor.

I scanned the names of the performers on each of the dressing room doors until I came to Roxy's. I waited outside listening hard. It was difficult to make out what was being said, but I didn't have time to eavesdrop. I took the rod from my pocket and kicked open the door.

Roxy was on the far side of the room. Venice, her back to me, was blocking my view. Did she have a gun? Was she squirting lead? I really didn't have a sheridan. So I leaped at her, grabbing her waist and dragging her to the ground.

"Get security!" called someone. Someone I hadn't seen, who'd been standing behind the door. In fact there was more than one

## Chapter 17

someone – a cameraman, a man with a boom microphone that he was now smashing against me and another with a clipboard, who was now sitting on my head.

Venice dusted herself down and stared down at me in disbelief.

"Jack! What the f..." Professional to the last, she looked round at the camera and paused "blazes are you doing?"

She had no gat. I couldn't believe it. I had it flat that she'd have her dame-pistol in her hand.

"You really weren't about to pop her?" I murmured.

"Christ Jack, I'm her mentor – I was just going over her performance. Live, you know, in front of half the nation."

As I was dragged out along the corridor, it sunk in. Live TV! I was going to be up there in the great TV moments alongside the Beatles on *Sullivan*, the moment they told us Nixon's office was bugged and Janet Jackson's Superbowl nipple – "The idiot who toppled Venice Budgetlodge."

The timbernecks had given me the bounce as far as reception when Snarling's voice came over their walkie-talkie. He didn't sound pleased. "I want that Schitt locked in a room, until I've got time to deal with him..."

When the guard grabbed his own radio to reply, I lammed off. They chased me through the car park but I lost them round the back of the building. I could really do with them not getting gashouse on me, my scars hadn't healed from the last beating yet. To get the heat off my back, I climbed a dumpster and launched myself in. I could fade in here a while – if I could stand the smell of the rotting catering refuse.

## Chapter 18: Payback

In the dark of the dumpster, I tried to imagine how the show would progress. They'd pretend that my little cameo hadn't happened and carry on regardless. Roxy would probably win - saps ringing in their droves to vote for her in sympathy for having to witness a grown man flying in through her dressing room door and knocking her mentor to the floor.

I leaned back and felt a slop of coleslaw trickle down the back of my neck. I could have sworn I'd already put my size 10 into a chicken carcass – all I needed now was some potato salad in my coat pocket for the whole meal deal. This LA trip hadn't really worked out, had it? A hardened dick hiding amidst the food waste of a TV studio?

And what of Snarling? He was an arrogant asshole for sure, but he'd given me a chance and I'd blown it big time. He deserved some kind of apology but if I showed my face I could end up back at Chzopski's all-nighter.

I decide to lay low – just try to turn myself away from the fish side of the oversize trash can. After an hour or so, I heard the coaches and cars engines starting up – the audience had had their hit of euphoria and were heading back to suburbia to carry on their mundane lives. It was dark now and I was able to wipe the eggshell from my hair and

## Chapter 18

lift my noddle out of the bin. The last cars were disappearing. Snarling and the others would be heading for the after-show party by now.

I waited another hour before emerging . It wasn't exactly a hell-hole in Vietnam, but it felt good to be out. I stretched my runners, smoothed out my rags and headed for the exit – keeping smart for the studio goons. Then, I slowed and halted. I don't know if it was the actions of a gee wanting to do the right thing, whether I wanted to prove I was no sap or if I was just being a right abercrombie – but I turned heels and headed for Snarling's office. I'd just leave a note – sorry it didn't work out, kind of thing.

The offices were all in darkness by now – everyone was down at the party – but I had my little penknife torch and knew my way to Snarling's box. The door was locked but I'd opened easier cans for supper – a couple of clicks with the knife and I was in. I went to his desk. I just needed a pen and notepaper and I could skedaddle.

Before I could even put pen to paper, I heard someone else's mitt on the door handle. Damn. I jumped back behind the curtains, hoping Snarling had just nipped back to fetch something. But it wasn't the oily-faced slimebag at all – it was Venice! She had no torch but was looking for something – turning drawers out and going through the shelves. She was getting frustrated and desperate, hurling things onto the floor. This was all too peachy for me – it was time I revealed myself and found out what was going down. I put one hand on my Beretta and placed a foot outside the curtain.

It was as if I'd pressed a switch with my loafer. The lights came on. I pulled my foot back. It was Snarling. This sure beat an episode of *Forensic Unit*, even that uneventful one set in Vancouver.

"Ah, Venice," his smooth tones sounded un-alarmed. "Looking for anything particular or just trashing my office for the fun of it – Jesus! What's that smell – is that you?"

Her voice was the opposite, flustered and panicked. "You know what I want Mark – the disc that your man with the head mark stole."

He still sounded cool. "Borrowed," he corrected her. "It's interesting viewing". I heard the TV come on and a familiar voice come from the speaker.

"Hi daddy, it's me." It was a sugary sweet Venice. "I know you've been angry with me and won't talk to me so I thought I'd make you this tape to explain." Snarling spoke over the next bit. "Very moving this," he said. "I haven't cried so much since *Titanic* and you're much less wooden than Kate Winslet. You should do a movie, sweetheart."

"The sex tapes – they're all faked daddy – it's just my career." Venice on tape continued. " I'm still what you'd call 'pure', daddy – I promise. Look I'll show you how it's done, I've got this studio in my apart..."

I peered through the gap in the curtains – catching a brief glimpse of the room in which I made my porn debut. So Venice had been faking it all just for the headlines, but hadn't realized daddy would write her out of his will. This must have been her desperate attempt to win him back before he croaked.

Meanwhile, the action had been cranked up in my private drama. Venice had pulled her baby pistol.

"Yeah great Mark, just eject it and pass it over."

The thought flashed through my mind. I was right, she had killed Mel and Jas. OK, I was wrong about Roxy, it was Snarling she was after next. I knew what to do, just like in the films I'd quietly step out, put the shooter to her pretty neck and whisper.

"Give me the heater, babe – we don't need another stiff in the show."

Which would have been good. Instead, my phone went.

## Chapter 18

Damn, it was mom! I hadn't spoke to her for days, she'd be worried sick but this wasn't the time or place. I glanced down, feverishly trying to reject the call.

The ringtone had ruined the surprise. My appearance didn't create the impact I'd anticipated. "Oh, it's just Jack," said Venice. Snarling looked to the heavens, "Chrissakes, not you again – and look at you, you smell like a hobo's gusset."

Venice looked at my shooter and smiled. "That's a big one Jack!" she said smiling. Did the broad never give it up? But in an instant, Snarling jumped over and grabbed the pistol from Venice's paw.

"Call the cops, Jack," ordered Snarling. "She's off the tracks, this one."

As I reached deep into my pocket for my phone, I felt my flipper shake and a noise rip through the air. Snarling fell to the ground, screaming. I looked at the Beretta – it was still smoking. I'd done it again. Shot him straight through the foot.

"Call the paramedics, Jack," he said through the pain. I looked at my phone. I just had to press the numbers – but where were the numbers? These confounded phones, I thought. The screen said "Last call: Mom"; at the top there was a note saying "missed calls 13" and there was a tape symbol. In a panic, I pressed the last one.

"You have one message and one saved message," it began. How do I stop it?

"Message Two: Hi just Mom, I'm worried about you son – give me a call."

"Message One..."

"Hurry," cried Jack, "I'm bleeding to death here." Venice was wrapping a scarf around his ankle to stop the blood. The message player continued...

## Payback

"Jack! Where are you? It's Jas – Mark's in the launderette – he's got a gun! Help me please." Then there was the sound of a shot and a scream. I'd have just been talking to my mum around then.

It had played loud enough for the others to catch it too. Venice looked up at me. She grabbed the phone, pressed some buttons (I wouldn't have known how) and the message came over again – this time through a speaker, so that we all could hear.

We both looked at Snarling. He winced through the pain in his foot.

"I loved her Jack. She wanted to leave me... I couldn't face her going. The most powerful man in TV and she thought she could just walk out like that – after I'd..."

Venice was ahead of me, she guessed what was coming next:

"After you'd killed Mel for her? So she could win the show? Oh God, Mark how could you? Oh my God."

My gunfire had been heard through the building. By now a crowd had gathered, Danny and Euston stood by the door, looking down at Venice holding Snarling in his arms.

"What's that smell babe?" he asked Euston.

Chzopski pushed his way to the front. Looked at the mess on the floor and up at me

"Oh not you again," he spat. Then he sniffed. "Is that fish, Schitt?"

"Just doing your job for you," I replied, walking to the door. I looked back at Snarling. "Someone better call the paramedics," I murmured.

Euston stepped forward, picking up a pink phone from Snarling's desk. She pressed a button, frowned and turned to Danny. "Dan? Danny? Isn't that your tattoo?"

The crowd around the door split like the Red Sea – in awe of my work, or because of the smell, I couldn't tell – and I walked right through. I didn't look back.

## Epilogue: The Damned Don't Cry

```
There was no one to wave me off at the airport.
Snarling was occupied at the big house; Venice
was busy pretending to do the whoopty-do while
making nice with her daddy; Bendham was under
house arrest by his wife; and Chzopski was
still wondering how some schmuck from the
sticks had fronted out the case. Everyone else
was dead.
```

By time I got back to my office in Mazomanie, my mom had already left a flask of Joe, a copy of the *Trumpet* and a round of pastrami and gherkin on rye. I settled in my chair, poured a cup of the Java and pressed the button on my answerphone. There was just one call:

"Hi there! My name's Dane and I'm calling from WNXZ News in LA. I'm not sure if I've got the right number, you don't know Jack Schitt do you?"

I stopped the message and picked up the copy of the *Trumpet*.